P9-CSW-171

*S*ighing, I ran both thumbs down his face. "Jude Ryder. What am I going to do with you?" I asked.

It was, perhaps, the question to end all questions. Nothing was easy about our relationship. Well, nothing but falling hard for each other. Everything else was like trying to fight an uphill battle. You never felt like you were making much headway, but the journey made up for the lack of ground you covered.

Latching onto my hips, Jude planted me back down on the ground. He spun me around, and his fingers worked the satin ribbon free of the last rivets. His hands just barely skimmed my skin, but "just barely" shot bursts of heat deep into my stomach.

"What am *I* going to do with *you*, Luce?" he threw back at me, his voice carefully controlled.

Also by
NICOLE WILLIAMS

CRASH
CRUSH

NICOLE WILLIAMS
CLASH

Simon & Schuster

First published in Great Britain in 2012 as eBook original
by Simon & Schuster UK Ltd
This paperback edition published in 2013 by Simon & Schuster UK Ltd
A CBS COMPANY

Copyright © 2012 Nicole Williams

This book is copyright under the Berne Convention.
No reproduction without permission.
All rights reserved.

The right of Nicole Williams to be identified as the author of this work
has been asserted by her in accordance with sections 77 and 78
of the Copyright, Designs and Patents Act, 1988.

1 3 5 7 9 10 8 6 4 2

Simon & Schuster UK Ltd
1st Floor, 222 Gray's Inn Road
London
WC1X 8HB

Simon & Schuster Australia, Sydney
Simon & Schuster India, New Delhi

A CIP catalogue record for this book is available from the British Library.

eBook ISBN: 978-1-47111-762-6
PB ISBN: 978-1-47111-763-3

*This book is a work of fiction. Names, characters, places and incidents
are either the product of the author's imagination or are used fictitiously.
Any resemblance to actual people living or dead,
events or locales is entirely coincidental.*

Printed and bound in Australia by Griffin Press

www.simonandschuster.co.uk
www.simonandschuster.com.au

Dedicated to all the lovely fans, book bloggers, and author friends who made Crash *what it is and wouldn't rest until I gave Jude and Lucy another chapter in their story. I'm thankful to you all in ways I'll never be able to repay.*

ONE

You know how they say it's always darkest before the dawn? Well, I'd lived five years of dark. I'd done my time—*hard* time—and I was officially done in on all things dark. I was ready for my dawn, and as I danced across the stage, I realized I was finally living my dawn.

I didn't let myself focus on the one thousand people who were watching me. Progressing into the difficult finale, I danced for only one. The lights that blinded me to the crowd, the pressure to perform that drove me forward, and the wardrobe malfunction that was one thread from snapping away—I pushed it all aside and danced for him.

As I took my final grand allegro into the air, my pointes landed at the exact moment the music came to a close.

This was it. The moment I loved. The breath and a half

of stillness and silence before I moved into a curtsy and the crowd applauded. A two-second window to reflect and revel in the blood, sweat, and tears I'd shed to get to this point. *Job well done, Lucy Larson.*

It was a moment I wanted to last forever, but I accepted it for what it was. A glimpse at perfection before it was swept away.

Sucking in a breath, I lifted my arms, and moving into curtsy position, I lifted my eyes. Right where Madame Fontaine had trained me to direct them at the conclusion of a performance. Front and center. A smile played at the corners of my mouth.

It was impossible not to smile when Jude Ryder sat front and center.

He leaped up from his seat, clapping like he was trying to fill the whole room with it, grinning at me in a way that made my stomach tighten. People were already peering over with curiosity, so when Jude jumped onto his seat and began hooting "Bravo" at top volume, those looks of curiosity got more judgmental.

Not that I cared. I'd learned a while back that being with Jude meant going up against the norm. It was a cost worth paying to be with him.

Taking one more curtsy, I met his gaze again and did the unthinkable. Thank the maker Madame Fontaine hadn't been here tonight, because her perpetually tight bun might have just busted something. I aimed a wink right at my man towering over the crowd, cheering for me like I'd just the saved the world.

The lights fell, and before I hurried offstage, I heard one more round of Jude hooting and whistling. He was breaking every unspoken rule of how to show appreciation for the arts. I loved it.

We did things totally outside the box, our relationship included.

"Think you could try, just for once, not to give a perfect performance? You know, so the rest of us don't look like such bush leaguers," Thomas, a fellow student and dancer, whispered at me as I scurried behind the curtains.

"I could," I whispered back as the last dancer took the stage. "But where's the fun in that?"

Smirking, he tossed me a bottle of water. Catching it with one hand, I waved it in thanks and headed to the dressing room to stretch and change. I had a ten-minute window before the performance would draw to a conclusion, and I knew from experience Jude would be barreling backstage to find me if I didn't find him first. He wasn't exactly a patient man, especially following a dance recital. My ultimate turn-on was watching him play football—his was watching me dance.

Sliding into the dressing room, I grabbed my foot, stretching my quad while I hopped over to my corner of the room, untying my pointe. The elastic band holding my corset in place so my performance didn't turn into a peep show snapped the moment I stretched my neck to the side. My wardrobe couldn't have picked a better time to "malfunction."

As I stretched the other leg back, my fingers worked to undo my other pointe. Tossing both shoes into my bag, I pulled out my jeans, sweater, and riding boots. It was Friday night, and since Jude had a home game tomorrow, that meant we got the whole night to ourselves. He had something planned, and he'd told me to dress warm. I would have rather been dressing for warm weather, but really, when it came to being with Jude, I didn't care what I was wearing. In fact, I would have preferred to wear nothing, but the latest patron saint of virtue, Jude Ryder, wasn't having any of that until he "figured his shit out."

I'd never wanted shit to get figured out faster.

I really needed to stretch a little longer, but I had two minutes max before Jude would come bursting through the dressing room door. Twisting my arms behind me, I worked away at my corset. Where was Eve, our costumer, when I needed her? That girl could fasten and unfasten a costume faster than a playa could lower his zipper in the backseat of his sports car.

I was searching for a pair of scissors to escape the satin straitjacket when a warm set of hands rested over my shoulders.

"May I be of assistance?" Thomas said, grinning at me as I looked over my shoulder.

"If your assistance comes with speed and precision, then yes, please," I replied.

His smile turned wicked. "When it comes to removing women's clothing, speed and precision are my top priorities."

I elbowed him as he laughed. "Anytime today, Mr. Hot Fingers."

"Yes, ma'am," he said, cracking his fingers dramatically before moving to the back of my dress.

Thomas was right—he had the undressing maneuver down pat. However, there was nothing even remotely intimate about one dancer helping another dancer dress or undress, male or not. You danced long enough, you got used to about every dancer in a three-state radius seeing you next to naked. There was no room for being a prude in the world of dance.

"Almost," Thomas murmured as his fingers worked toward the bottom rivet of my corset.

I was about to spit something witty back when the dressing room door flew open.

"What the hell?" he hollered, his face flaming red.

"Jude," I began.

"You're a dead man," he yelled, lunging toward Thomas.

Dodging in front of Jude, I pressed my hands into his brick wall of a chest.

"Jude!" This time I yelled. "Stop!" I put my arms around Jude to give Thomas a chance to retreat.

"Sure, I'll stop," Jude replied, his silver eyes flashing onyx. "Once this tool is dancing across the stage in a wheelchair."

I hadn't seen his rage monster in months. I was rendered speechless. Momentarily. This was the kind of anger people told stories about.

Jude gently removed my arms. Pivoting around me, he charged at Thomas, who was staring wide-eyed, half-confused, half-terrified, at the bull of a man trying to obliterate him. My strength was no match for Jude, not even a tenth of a match, but I had other powers that could render him into servitude. Sprinting in front of him, I jumped, wrapping my arms and legs around him as tight as they would go.

He stilled instantly, the murderous look dimming. Just barely.

"Jude," I said calmly, waiting for his eyes to shift to mine. They did. "Stop," I repeated.

I pointed to Thomas. "He was helping me get out of my costume. I asked him to. I wanted to hurry and get changed so I could be with *you*," I emphasized, "and unless you wanted to wait a year and a half for me, you should be thanking Thomas."

Jude now directed his glare at me. "Why didn't you have me help, Luce?" he asked, his jaw clenching.

"Because you weren't here," I said, feeling like I was stating the obvious, but if obvious was what it took to talk Jude down from the ledge, so be it.

"I'm here now."

I stroked his cheeks. "Yes, you are," I said, waiting for his eyes to lighten up completely. His chest was starting to lift and fall in a regular pattern again. "Thanks for the *help*, Thomas." I glanced back at Thomas, who was still staring at Jude like he was about to go all nuclear on him again. "Catch up with you later?"

Thomas sidestepped around us, never taking his eyes off Jude. "Sure, Lucy," he said. "Catch up with you later."

I smiled my appreciation. "Good night."

"Bye, Peter Pan," Jude called after him. "I'll 'catch up with you later' too."

Thomas was already out the dressing room door, but there was no doubt he'd heard Jude's latest bout of name-calling threats.

Sighing, I ran both thumbs down his face. "Jude Ryder. What am I going to do with you?" I asked.

It was, perhaps, the question to end all questions. Nothing was easy about our relationship. Well, nothing but falling hard for each other. Everything else was like trying to fight an uphill battle. You never felt like you were making much headway, but the journey made up for the lack of ground you covered.

Latching onto my hips, Jude planted me back down on the ground. He spun me around, and his fingers worked the satin ribbon free of the last rivets. His hands just barely skimmed my skin, but "just barely" shot bursts of heat deep into my stomach.

"What am *I* going to do with *you*, Luce?" he threw back at me, his voice carefully controlled.

"Since you've almost got me topless, I'll let you fill in the blanks to that question," I teased, arching a brow at him.

His eyes weren't liquid like they usually were when we were sharing an intimate moment. The corners of his mouth weren't twitching in anticipation. Jude was all Mr. Stern on me.

"Don't do that again, Luce," he said, folding the ribbon in his hands before stuffing it into his pocket.

"What?" I said with a shrug. I feigned ignorance, but I

was starting to boil. I didn't like being talked down to, especially by Jude.

"You know what."

I put my frown on. "Since I've obviously disappointed you, I wouldn't want to do it again, so why don't you spell it out for me?"

I cursed myself. The only thing that would result from fighting fire with fire would be some nasty first-degree burns. Jude and I didn't need our relationship to get any more complicated, so why was I pounding on complicated's door?

Sucking in a slow breath, I witnessed the effort it took for him to stay calm. He was making the effort to keep this from blowing up into a screaming match—why wasn't I?

"Don't let another man, tight-wearing fairy or not, help you out of your clothes again," he said, his eyes narrowing. "If you need help getting out of so much as a sock, you call me, you got it? That's my job."

Super. The possessive, overbearing police were back in town. He could deny it all he wanted, but overbearing implied he didn't trust me. Call me a fool, but trust wasn't only pivotal to a relationship, it was everything.

"Got it, Luce?" he said when I stayed quiet.

God, I loved him. Too much for my own good, but I would not let him order me around.

"No, Jude. I don't 'got it,'" I said, about to blow a gasket. "So why don't you go wait outside and let that sink in while I finish getting undressed?

"Alone," I added before he could open his mouth to object. Because if he did, I wouldn't be able to say no.

He paused, indecision written on his face. Finally, he nodded. "Okay," he said. "I'll be right outside."

"Is that so you can scare off any other guys who might help me with my costume, or just because you're waiting patiently and respectfully for your girlfriend?" I said, heading over to my bag.

Jude's sigh was as long as it was tortured. "Both," he said, his voice just above a whisper before he closed the door behind him.

As soon as he was gone, I felt it. Guilt. Remorse. Followed up by a potent dose of regret.

I knew what I was getting into when Jude and I got back together at the start of our first year of college. I went in willingly with both eyes open; I'd gladly gone in. Jude had been through more shit than any one person should, and along with that came certain characteristics that could be classified as extreme.

But you took the bad with the good. And when it came to Jude Ryder Jamieson, there was a surplus of good that always managed to not necessarily wipe the bad clean, but to make it a fair trade. If I was pointing fingers at damaged goods, I might as well turn that finger around. I was a far cry from flawless.

That was the beauty of us being together. And the problem.

I had as many triggers that ticked at my temper and as many ghosts from my past as Jude did. When his anger flamed, mine responded in kind, and vice versa. As in the last two minutes.

Then, as it always did, the anger I'd felt toward Jude shifted toward me. If I'd taken a time-out to take a step inside Jude's size twelve Cons, what would I have said or done if I'd walked in on some girl assisting him out of his clothes?

Shrugging into my sweater, I realized my reaction would not have been that far off from his. In fact, my claws would have been mid-swipe before he could open his mouth to explain. The old Jude, the one pre-Lucy, would have kicked ass first and asked questions later. The new Jude, although still not an anger management graduate, had allowed words to defuse the situation, not fists.

Progress. Significant progress he'd made for me. And how had I repaid it?

By yelling at him and throwing him out of the dressing room.

Tossing the rest of my clothes on, I stuffed my costume into my bag. I didn't bother letting my hair out of its headache-inducing bun. I didn't wash off the three-layer-deep pancake makeup covering my face.

I had to get to him. I couldn't get to Jude fast enough.

I threw the door open.

Leaning against the opposite wall, Jude was every shade of tormented. The emotion expressing itself on his face was the exact emotion I was sweltering in.

One side of his mouth curved up as he rubbed the back of his neck.

Dropping my bag, I rushed to him, wrapping both arms around him so tightly I could feel every one of his ribs hard against my chest. He embraced me with just as much urgency and maybe even more relief.

"I'm sorry," I said, inhaling the boy who, even in scent, exuded a hint of trouble just barely masked by a reluctant sweetness.

Tucking my head under his chin, he exhaled. "I'm sorry, too."

TWO

"Why won't you tell me where we're going?" I asked, squeezed next to Jude on the bench seat of his old truck so that every inch of me ran against most every inch of him.

He smiled at the dark road we were bouncing over. Wherever we were going, our country surroundings suggested there wouldn't be modern conveniences like hot water and cell phone reception.

"Because I'm enjoying your attempts to pull it from me far too much," he answered, glancing over at me. His eyes sparkled with wicked joy.

My heart did the sputter-to-a-stop thing. Right before it restarted like it was trying to take flight. "Is that so?"

He made a noise of agreement while licking his lips.

Against every instinct drilled into me by driver's ed, I

snapped out of my seat belt and slid across the seat until I was pressed up against the passenger-side window. "Still enjoying yourself?"

He looked over at me, his face lined, right before he reached across the seat for me. "Where do you think you're going?" he asked, sliding me back across the seat, but he didn't stop there. Grabbing my right thigh, he lifted it, shifting me until my hips had successfully landed over his lap. The truck didn't slow, it sped up, so that my body vibrated above Jude's.

"I guess I'm not going anywhere," I whispered, lacing my fingers together behind his neck, feeling the steering wheel against my back, feeling the firmness of his body everywhere else.

He kept one eye on the road and one hand on the steering wheel, but the rest of his body was focused on me. "Damn right, you're not," he said, his mouth curving into a smile that disappeared when my mouth covered his.

It wasn't quite a moan—it went deeper than that—but the sound that came from his chest when my lips parted his and my tongue crept into his mouth was all Jude. I wasn't paying the truck that much attention, but I thought I might have detected another increase in speed.

Jude kissed me back, matching every slide of my tongue and movement of my lips with his own. His free hand slid beneath my sweater, traveling up my back. It was warm, slightly rough from days spent working in the garage and on the football field.

The truck hit a particularly nasty bump, slamming my lap down hard against his. Heat spread from the area between my legs, and this time it was me who made a noise that came from somewhere deep within. The dangerous reality of us driving down a dark, gravel country road at thirty to forty miles an hour didn't quite sink in when my hands left his neck to tug at the hem of my sweater. If he wasn't going to do it, I was. Throwing the sweater over my head, I tossed it across the bench seat.

"Luce," Jude said, his voice just enough strained to let me know I was doing something very right. "I'm trying to drive here."

He'd put the brakes on this too many times before, meta-phorically speaking—I wasn't letting him this time.

Moving my mouth just outside his ear, I whispered, "Me too," right before I took his earlobe into my mouth, sucking it softly.

Another sound slid up his throat, this one so loud it caused his chest to vibrate against mine. "Hell with it," he said, no hesitation or uncertainty in his voice. It was as firm and resolute as his body thrumming beneath mine.

With one flick of his fingers, my bra snapped open,

sliding down my arms until it landed on the floor beside Jude's feet. His mouth covered mine again, hot and unyielding. I couldn't breathe. I didn't want to if it meant not being able to kiss Jude like he was kissing me right now. How he could make me feel his passion, his love, and his possession in one kiss was inexplicable. But he could. Jude's body expressed his feelings better than his words did.

"A little help?" he breathed in between kisses. His hand grabbed mine and lifted it to the top button of his shirt. "Unless you want to finish this thing in the hospital, I've got to keep one hand on the wheel." His words were strained, like I knew mine would be if I could talk right now. "I want to feel you against me, Luce," he said when my fingers forgot what they were supposed to be doing.

Even with both hands fumbling with it, it took me one long kiss to get the first button freed. I was a graceful girl— except when being intimate with Jude. Here, I became a klutzy mess of nerves and limbs. Realizing we'd be across the state line before I finished the job, I stopped kissing him so I could focus. A *bit* more.

The way he looked at me as I pulled away rendered me almost useless.

"Are you sure this is safe?" I asked, forcing myself to take a controlled breath. I had to replace and store as much oxygen as my lungs were capable of before getting back to Jude.

"Not that I really care, but I'm sure we're breaking about every traffic law ever, and I did kind of make you promise to stay on the straight and narrow." Two more buttons free, a few more to go.

I grinned—it was the little things that made me happy.

Jude's smile evened out as both eyes met mine for an instant. "Of course you're safe, Luce," he promised, his glance shifting back to the road. "I would never put you in harm's way. I would never let anything happen to you," he said, like it was a mantra. "You know that. Right?"

Leave it to Jude to take a simple question and to twist it into a heavy "issue" talk.

"Of course I do," I said, looking up at him before focusing on the next button. I wasn't letting the turn in conversation stop me. "I was just checking. Straddling a driver while we attempt to undress each other at forty miles per hour is a first for me. Just wanted to get the safety seal of approval before proceeding."

"This better be a first," he said, the seriousness of before fading. "And consider your safety seal stamped. I was driving before I was jerking off, Luce. I can control a vehicle better than I can control myself."

"Baby," I said, freeing the last button right before I tugged the shirt free from his pants, "your words never fail to make me want to swoon and squirm at the same time."

Pulling his shirt from his body, I slid my chest against his. The soft parts of my body molded to the hard parts of his. The lightest sheen of sweat was covering his chest, mixing with the glow on mine. Another uptick of the speedometer arrow.

"I wouldn't want to disappoint you, Luce," he said, his free hand clamping tight around my back.

This was the furthest he'd let things get since last spring, right before we graduated and discovered how our families' pasts tragically wove together. My body had forgotten how to breathe—I had to remind myself how to do it.

"You never do," I whispered through a smile as my hands moved down the cut ridges of his stomach, settling on the seam of his jeans. Now *this* button my fingers managed to tug free in the time it took for one surprised inhalation from Jude.

"Luce." There was warning in his voice, but also welcoming.

I chose to hear the latter.

Pinching his zipper between my thumb and finger, I slid it down, torn between wanting to savor the moment and wanting to let it devour me whole. Done with the zipper, I folded the material of his jeans down and slid over him once more, until I could feel his body warmth between my legs.

He groaned, moving beneath me, making me gasp out loud.

"Dammit," he muttered as both arms wound tight around me right before he slammed the brakes. His arms held me firmer than any seat belt could have.

"I thought you could handle it," I said, smirking at him.

His chest rising and falling hard against mine, he met my smirk with one of his own. "I was wrong."

And then his mouth was on mine, his hands cupping my face. His body pushed against mine, arching my back over the steering wheel.

"Yes?" I managed to get out. It was a one-word question, and he didn't need any further explanation. It was one I'd been asking for a while. One he'd never agreed to, up until tonight.

I felt his smile against my mouth as his tongue teased mine for another moment. He held my face as firmly as one could and still be considered gentle; his mouth pulled back, and his eyes met mine.

"Hell yes," he replied, but his smile conveyed anticipation and conflict.

Every muscle in my body clenched in anticipation. This was it. Finally. The guy who'd slept with more girls than I cared to know about was finally permitting himself to sleep with his girlfriend.

"Are you sure?" he asked, looking like he'd bust something if I answered in the negative.

"I'm so sure I went on the pill the week after we got back together," I said, sliding up and down over his lap. He groaned again, his head falling back against the seat. "Are you sure?" I asked, moving a bit faster to sway his response.

"Luce, I'm so sure I went and got tested and have been carrying this condom around in my back pocket since the *day* we got back together," he said, grinning that tortured grin at me.

I put my hands on his face, tracing with my thumb the scar that ran down the length of his cheek. He was everything I wanted—in every way a girl could want a guy—and at last, I could have him the one way I hadn't.

"I love you, Jude," I said. Because that was all there was left to say.

"And that makes me the luckiest bastard in the world."

I smiled at him. "Come here," I said, holding his face while lowering my mouth to his. "I want to know how the luckiest bastard in the world makes love."

"Yes, ma'am," he said before fitting his lips to mine.

His hands had just found their way to the button of my jeans when a blinding set of headlights exploded into the front of Jude's car.

I groaned, covering my eyes with one forearm and my

chest with the other when the driver flicked the truck's brights on.

"Shit," Jude cursed, squinting over his shoulder.

The truck door blasted open, followed by some male hooting and shouting.

"Expecting company?" I sighed, covering my bare chest with my other arm too as I worked my way off his lap. It was painful, separating myself from the what-could-have-been.

"Not exactly," he replied, folding himself over my lap and grabbing my sweater. Lifting it over my head, he pulled it on, holding each arm for me as I worked my way into it. The sweater felt scratchier than it had five minutes ago. He was angry, that was evident across every plane of his face, but he was keeping it contained. He was controlling the beast, not letting it control him.

Jude had just zipped his pants when someone threw himself against the driver's-side door.

"Ryder, man!" one of Jude's teammates hollered through the window, looking the two of us up and down. "You getting your freak on with your woman?" Looking at me, Jude's teammate wagged his brows. "You lucky bastard."

Glancing my way, Jude smirked at me. "Told you."

A fire crackled at my feet, the stars blinked above me, Jude's arms held me tight against him, and the sound of an entire college football team belching their way through "Hey, Jude" serenaded me.

"I can't believe this big night I thought you'd planned for us also involved over fifty football players," I said, tilting my head back against Jude's chest and looking up at him so he could see my expression. Jude hadn't left my side since his teammates showed up, except to pee in the woods once.

"Sorry, babe," he said, kissing the lines of my forehead. "I thought we'd have a couple hours to ourselves before these animals showed up."

A couple hours? I would have settled for about fifteen minutes.

The belching chorus came to an inconclusive ending, the temporary silence only to be interrupted by a chorus of farting. I groaned, closing my eyes and pinching my nose.

"Man, that was lame, Ryder." Tony, Jude's number one wide receiver, yelled across the campfire. "If I was trying to win a girl back, there's no way I'd go through the whole effort of bribing her roommate to get her to some mixer so I could have the DJ serenade her with some suck-ass oldies song while I professed my undying love."

I opened my eyes so I could shoot a glare at Tony. I loved the guy—it was impossible not to, most days. This wasn't one of those days.

"I'd just go up to her and be like, 'Hey, baby. How's it

going?' You know, something real smooth like that?" Tony smiled like the devil at me.

"Tony," Jude spoke up, curling his chin over my shoulder, "when was the last time you got one of your old girlfriends to take your sorry ass back?"

Tony's face scrunched up. Shrugging, he answered, "Never."

"Exactly," Jude said, lifting his middle finger at him.

My arms were tucked tight into the blanket Jude had wrapped me in, so when he lowered his finger, I nudged him. "One more for me."

Tony got the finger from Jude again, this one courtesy of Lucy Larson.

"Come on, Lucy," Tony said as the rest of the players shook in laughter, a few showering him in marshmallows. "You know I think you're the shit. I'm just jealous because you're about five times too good for Ryder, and I want to get in on that five-times-too-good-for-me action too."

"Maybe if you stopped dropping the ball and started getting it into the end zone, you could manage to find a girl who'd deign to lower her standards for you," I said, cocking my head.

Jude stifled his laughter into the blanket. The rest of the team, not so much.

Raising his brows at me, Tony slid the sleeve of his

T-shirt up, kissing his grotesquely large bicep, then did the same to the other one. "Stop hating on me, Lucy. Jude's going to catch onto us if you don't stop being so obvious," he said, ducking his head as Jude's mostly full sports drink bottle sailed past him. "And no need to worry about the end zone tomorrow, baby. I'm making that end zone my bitch."

"I won't hold my breath," I replied, no longer able to contain my smile at Tony's theatrics. At any given time, he was like watching a one-man three-ring circus. And, all jesting aside, Tony was one hell of a wide receiver. Together, he and Jude had been setting records that probably wouldn't be challenged anytime soon.

"Here's what I don't get," Tony said, nudging the guy next to him, the team's number one kicker. I think his name was Kurt. Or maybe it was Kirk. Or Kent. K something. "In the appearance department, Ryder's a seven, maybe an eight," he said, narrowing his eyes as he inspected Jude. Kurt or Kirk appraised Jude, rubbing his chin.

"Then you're a negative two, Tony," I muttered, really cursing the gods that I was stuck bantering with a couple of Jude's teammates tonight.

"His personality gets a negative ten," Tony continued. "So why, in all things unfair and unholy, does he get all the good ones lining up outside his door?"

24

Jude leaned forward. "I can give you an eight-inch explanation, Rufello."

Tony and the kicker stared at Jude, then each other, right before their heads tipped back and they erupted with laughter.

Jude joined in about halfway through.

But something Tony said needed clarification. "What good ones are lining up outside Jude's door?" I asked, trying to keep my voice even.

Tony's laughter trailed off, his dark eyes shifting away as soon as they landed on me. Jude's body stiffened just enough around me to indicate something was off.

"You," Tony said, gesturing in my direction. "You're the 'good ones' lining up outside his door."

Nope, I wasn't buying it. I'd seen Tony close to tears the night his senior year high school VIP trophy got snapped in half at one of the legendary parties at their house, and even then his smile was pretty much present. There wasn't a trace of it now, which meant Tony was working to cover something up.

"You," he repeated again, when I kept my eyes on his.

"And Adriana Vix," another one of Jude's teammates added behind us, sounding like he would be content to hook up with the name alone.

Now *my* body tensed, no longer fitting with Jude's. Twisting in my seat snuggled between his legs, I met his eyes.

Nothing in them gave anything away. That was the worst way they could be.

"Who's Adriana Vix?" I asked, my voice the perfect blend of anxious and pissed off.

Jude's hands cupped my face, staring straight into my eyes. It was hard to breathe when he looked at me like this. "No one," he answered, not removing his hands or looking away from me.

"No one?" the guy from behind us cried, taking a seat. "Your definition of 'no one' must be a girl most guys would amputate his limbs to be with. To be with *once*," the player continued. I couldn't remember his name, but I knew he rode the bench a lot. He was going to be permanently riding benches if he didn't shove the Adriana Vix worship where the sun didn't shine.

"Matt," Jude warned, finally letting my face go, but only to rewrap me into his arms, "shut up."

"Lucy was the one who asked," he replied, holding up his hands. "I was just answering a question."

"Well, stop embellishing," Jude said, his voice level, but I could sense his calm about to waver. "In fact, why don't you just stop talking for the rest of the night?"

Matt conceded with a shrug, taking a swig of his beer.

If it wasn't for the team's two-beer limit the night before a game, I could write off Matt's drooling over Adriana Vix as the ramblings of a drunk. Matt was sober, which meant Adriana was as hot as he was implying.

Turning so I could lean my back into the side of Jude's bent leg, I met his gaze again. He was wearing his old gray beanie tonight, but only because it was cold.

"She likes you?" Points to me for asking the question with as little emotion as possible.

He lifted a shoulder. "Maybe a little," he answered, his eyes never leaving mine.

"A little?" Tony said, as a handful of others smirked at us. "Thanks to Ryder, the male population of Syracuse has been enjoying even more of Adriana's goods on display. I thought they were about to pop out of that itty-bitty dress she showed up in yesterday." He whistled through his teeth, his eyes clouding in dreaminess. "That fine thing is on the prowl. And she's got her sights set on your man, love," he said, looking at me with a bit of pity. Like I'd already lost the game of Jude by default. Appearance default.

"Say that again, Tony," Jude warned, his jaw clenched, "and the only thing I'll be throwing at your pinhead again will be my boot."

"What?" Tony said. "Telling the truth about Adriana panting in heat for you?"

"No, shithead," Jude seethed, "Lucy is not your 'love.' She's mine. Only I get to call her that. Not some jerk-off with a big mouth."

There it was. The territorial Rottweiler that showed up when it came to me. Usually, it pissed me off when he talked about me like I was something that could be owned. But right now, after hearing about the goddess with "goods on display," I was fine with him going territorial.

"My bad," Tony said, rising and dusting off his pants. "Since I can't seem to keep my mouth shut, I better put myself to bed before I take a knuckle sandwich to the face." His mouth smiled at me, but his eyes didn't. There was still that hint of pity in them. Like I was about to be overthrown by Adriana Vix. "Get all your ugly, hairy butts to bed," Tony yelled at the last remaining stragglers staring with lidded eyes into the fire. "We've got some ass to kick tomorrow."

A chorus of grunts followed as most of the guys shoved themselves up and followed Tony into their respective tents or threw themselves across the tailgates of their trucks. This night was so not going how I'd imagined.

Jude and I sat huddled together in silence for a minute, both of us staring into the dimming fire, waiting for the other to say something first.

"Do you like her?" I whispered before I even realized I'd thought it.

Jude's sigh was long and irritated. It was the first time I could remember being relieved that he was irritated at me. Turning me around so I was facing him, but still sandwiched between his legs, he leveled those darkening eyes at me.

"No," he answered. "Not in the way your crazy mind is thinking."

He'd only caught a glimpse at how "crazy" my mind could get. "And what about in the other way?"

I watched the last flames of the fire's shadow dying on the side of Jude's jaw. "She's all right," he answered, lifting his brows and waiting. Because he knew me well enough to know something more was coming.

"She's all right?" I repeated, my voice going up. "She's all right in an I'd-screw-her-in-two-seconds-flat-if-I-was-single kind of way, or she's all right as in she's just some girl?"

Jude had warned me months ago not to ask questions I didn't want honest answers to. I instantly wished I could take my question back—sort of.

"Luce," Jude said, unwrapping the blanket cinched around me, grabbing my hands when he pulled them free, "you're my girl. *The* girl." A trace of pain flashed over his face. "When I look at Adriana, or any other girl for that matter, that's all I see. Some other girl who isn't *my* girl. I don't see them, Luce. I see you," he continued, his skin lining between his brows. "I've only ever seen you."

The worry clenching my stomach started to unravel.

"So could you please, for the love of God, cut out the paranoid girlfriend shit?"

With Jude, when he was like this, the best thing to do was cease and desist. I knew that, but couldn't ever seem to actually do it.

"Kind of like you didn't go all paranoid boyfriend on Thomas earlier tonight?"

Jude's mouth dropped open an inch. Clamping it shut, he frowned and leaned back into the log behind him. Face lined, eyes narrowed, teeth working at the right side of his cheek—this was a new expression of Jude's I'd become increasingly familiar with lately. It was his look of contemplation, the one he'd worked hard on to replace his gut reaction of anger.

I waited, giving him as much time as he needed.

"Luce," he said at last, his voice soft, "what do you want me to do?" He paused, waiting for my response, but I wasn't sure what he was asking, so I stayed quiet.

"Please, just tell me," he continued. "Tell me what you want me to say, and do, when it comes to Adriana or any other girl who looks my way, and I'll do it. You want me to fire a spit wad at their foreheads? You want me to flip them off anytime any one of them looks my way? You got it. You want me to poke my eyes out so I can't see another girl ever again?" He trailed off, grimacing. "Well, that would suck, but I'd do it. For you." Cradling my face in his hands again, he leaned forward so his eyes were staring into mine from half a foot away. "Just tell me, babe. What do you want me to do?"

I couldn't put it into words. When asked point-blank, I didn't even know what I wanted him to do or say when other girls got up in his business. Guys like Jude couldn't walk through a cemetery without being hit on. So what did I want from him when it came to the never-ending supply of girls ready and willing to throw themselves into his bed at the first chance? Did I want him to be an asshole? Well, yeah, kind of, but my reasonable self recognized this wasn't the answer. So what was?

That question would have to remain unanswered for now, because I had something else on my mind.

Lacing my fingers through his where they warmed my face, I scooted closer until I'd killed the half-foot space keeping us apart. "I want you to take me to bed."

I was sure I'd never seen the wrinkles creasing Jude's face disappear so quickly. "Anytime," he replied, scooping me into his arms before rising. "Any place."

I could have laughed if I'd let myself, but one name still hung between us. I wasn't ready to push pause on the Adriana Vix issue.

"Wait until you get a look at the setup I made for us,"

Jude said, his voice light as he carried me across the makeshift campground to his rusted-out truck. It was so rusted you couldn't tell if it'd originally been black or gray or some shade in between. He'd gotten the truck for next to nothing from some old farmer and had used part of the funds he made working at the garage to buy the parts it needed. The inside of the car was in fine working shape, but the outside looked like it needed to be junked.

I loved that Jude didn't care what anyone else but me thought. I loved how he'd said the inside was what counted. I knew he'd been talking about cars, his truck specifically, when he'd said it, but I'd still gone a little soft in the knees.

Weaving through a few of his teammates' new, souped-up monster trucks, Jude stopped at the back of his. He lowered the tailgate with one hand, and it screeched open. "Your room for the night, Miss Larson," he said in a singsong voice, motioning at the air mattress and mound of blankets and pillows lining the back of his truck. He'd even put a foil-wrapped chocolate on my pillow, right beside one white rose. I guessed this was what Jude was up to while he took his superlong pee break.

In high school, I'd learned what the colors of roses meant, and how you could decipher a guy's intentions based on what kind he gave you. Pink meant he had a crush on you, yellow meant he wanted to be friends—I couldn't count the number of abandoned yellow roses I'd seen decorating the insides of garbage cans in the high school halls—red meant he was in love, and white stood for purity.

Meaning his intentions were pure.

Meaning he didn't want to do all the things this girl was envisioning doing in the back of his truck bed tonight.

Damn all white roses to hell.

Despite my frustration, I kind of loved it, too. As soon as I thought I had Jude Ryder close to figured out, he went and left a white rose on my pillow. On the makeshift bed we'd be sharing a few hours after he'd just agreed to have sex with me practically on the steering wheel of his truck.

"You can be pretty romantic when you put your mind to it," I said, looking up at him.

"Don't tell anyone," he said, sitting me down on the tailgate. It creaked beneath me. "It would ruin my badass reputation. Plus, you think the girls are lining up now . . . ," he hinted, giving me a boyish smirk.

I shoved his chest; this reaction earned a chuckle from him.

So I decided to give him something he wasn't expecting. Grabbing two fistfuls of his thermal shirt, I pulled him to me.

"Come here," I whispered, lowering my gaze to his mouth. "Let me put those girls in their place."

His lips had just parted to kiss me when my mouth got there first. His hands gripped the flesh below my hips, sliding me to the edge of the tailgate so I was pressed right against him. At this angle, we were a perfect fit. That made me kiss him harder, my hands unable to explore him fast enough.

I could hear the quickened beating of Jude's heart. I could feel how every part of him wanted me. I could see the uncertainty eclipse his eyes when I wound my legs tight around his torso. I could sense the conflict stirring inside, reminding him that he was always careful with me, and I wanted to stop it in its tracks.

Grabbing the hem of his shirt, I tore it up his back, trying to rip it over his head.

Only to be stopped before it had made it past his chest.

"Yes?" I asked again, knowing his answer.

He didn't pause. "No," he said firmly. "Not like this."

I groaned so loudly I might have woken a couple of the guys closest to us. "Not like what? Hot, passionate, burning-the-night-away sex?"

Jude grinned so widely the scar on his cheek puckered. Gripping the tailgate, he worked on regulating his breathing.

"That sounds good," he said, catching his breath. Mine wouldn't be normal for at least another ten minutes. "But I'm not really into the kind where my girl is motivated to have sex with me because of jealousy over someone else. At least not for our first time," he said, pressing a soft kiss into my temple. "After that, I will gladly entertain and endure any and all jealous, angry sex you want to toss my way."

I shoved him again, resigned to this night taking a turn toward chaste. Kicking my boots off, I scooted back onto the air mattress.

Still grinning at me, Jude tossed his shoes off and leaped into the trunk. Tucking himself behind me, one arm wound under me and the other extended above me, holding out one white rose.

Jude laughed into the back of my neck.

I grabbed the rose and chucked it outside of the truck.

THREE

It was raining—or pouring. At least, that's what I thought as I drifted awake. Then I heard the muffled laughter and realized the reason my clothing and blankets clung to me sopping wet had nothing to do with Mother Nature.

I'd just opened my eyes when one of Jude's teammates, hovering over us on top of the cab, upended another huge bucket of water on Jude. Of course, it didn't *only* end up on him. I shrieked as the members of the football team erupted in laughter around Jude's truck. That was, until Jude lurched awake, taking a swing at the first guy who moved.

The player standing on his cab leaped off the truck before Jude could snag one of his ankles, but Jude was out of the bed and chasing him one second later. The poor guy wouldn't get far.

"Why you running, Clay?" Jude yelled after him, leaving a trail of water behind him. "We both know I'm a hell of a lot faster than you!"

Watching Jude close the gap between him and Clay, I wrung my hair out and threw the soggy blankets off to the side.

I made sure to glare at every last player standing there, even Tony, who was smiling at me with that boyish grin. He was already forgiven before he opened his mouth. "What?" he said, like I was overreacting. "Sorry, Lucy. But it's no fair Ryder got to stay warm last night snuggled up to your fine ass. We had to even up the playing field a bit."

Bouncing my way off the mattress, I threw myself over the tailgate. "Next time you boys decide to 'even the playing field' with Jude, could you please wait until I'm out of the truck?" I wanted to grab a blanket to wrap around me, but all of them were drenched. "It's freezing out here." My breath was fogging the air, making me shiver even more.

Tony's smile faded—just barely. "Ah, hell, Lucy," he said, shrugging out of his sweatshirt. "We're animals." Lifting his brows, he held his sweatshirt out to me like it was a peace offering. "Forgive us?"

Not in this lifetime, would have been my response had I been able to get it out around my chattering. I hated few things more than being cold—like maybe a root canal without novocaine.

Scowling at Tony, so he knew he wasn't totally off the hook, I grabbed the sweatshirt. It could have fit two normal-sized men with room to spare.

"Take this crap back." Appearing from behind me, Jude grabbed Tony's sweatshirt out of my hands and flung it at his face. "Next time you or any of you bastards do that again, I'm beating all your asses. You got that?" he hollered, his eyes sweeping over his teammates.

"And you," Jude said, stepping forward and putting his finger in Tony's face. "Don't you ever try to give Lucy something of yours to put on her body." The muscles just below Jude's neck were sticking out. "If you want me to throw another ball your way. Got that?"

And I thought *I'd* been pissed over a few gallons of water.

"Ryder," Tony said, lifting his hands in surrender.

Jude took another step at him until their chests were butting against each other. "You. Got. It?"

Tony dropped his eyes, taking a step back. "I got it."

"Good," Jude replied, turning toward me. The anger dissolved. "Let's get you some dry clothes," he said, his voice low and controlled.

I nodded. I didn't know how he could turn his anger on

and off like it was hot-wired to a switch, but it was as much a gift as it was a curse.

"Hey, Ryder," one of his teammates called after him. One of the ones who'd been on the outskirts and hadn't experienced a lethal dose of Jude fury. "What the hell did you do to Hopkins?"

Jude wrapped his arm around me, steering me toward the passenger side of his truck. "Locked him in your trunk, Palinski!"

When I peered up at him, he gave me his crooked smile.

"You didn't," I said, knowing he had.

"Hell yes, I did," he said, throwing open the door and leaning across the seat to retrieve his duffel bag. "And that's not the only payback that little douche is going to get today."

"Do I want to know?"

Shuffling through the contents of his bag, he pulled out a dark, long-sleeved shirt. "No. You don't," he answered, handing the shirt to me. "But you'll see."

Tucking the warm, dry shirt into my hands, I nodded. "Something to look forward to."

"Ryder," Tony said, clearing his throat as he stepped around the front of the truck. He was holding out his phone. "Coach just called. He wants us in an hour earlier than usual. I told him it would take us at least an hour to get back. He said we'd better haul ass." His face was almost a wince, like he was anticipating an explosive reaction from Jude.

"If Coach wanted us to be there an hour early, he should have told us sooner," Jude replied, not looking at him as he shuffled through some more contents in his bag. "I've got to get Luce some breakfast before taking her back to our place, so tell Coach I might be a few minutes late."

"You want me to tell him the reason you're going to be late?" Tony asked, nothing antagonistic in his voice.

"Damn straight I do," Jude said. "Tell him my girl comes before football. Tell him my girl's *breakfast* comes before football." Turning his gaze on Tony, he stared at him, waiting.

"You need me to write that down for you or you think you can handle that?" he added when Tony didn't reply.

"Nah," he said finally, managing a small smile. "Girl. Breakfast. Then football," he recited, tapping his head. "I think I got it."

Jude slammed the passenger-side door and came around the front of the truck. Pausing outside the driver's-side door, he peeled the wet thermal up and over his head and tossed it into the trees. Opening the door, he threw himself in and cranked the truck. Blasting the heaters, he pointed every one of them at me. I'd just been freezing cold, and now everything felt all gooey and warm, even though the heat hadn't kicked in yet. All because of one recently de-shirted man, wet and smiling beside me.

"What?" he said, his smile growing as I gazed at him.

Sweeping my eyes up his torso, I met his stare. I matched my smile to his. "Now that's a sight I like to wake up to in the morning."

After assuring Jude I in no way required a sit-down break-fast and that an egg-white sandwich and a hot cup of coffee would be more than sufficient, we pulled into the driveway of the house he and five other guys rented with enough time for him to make the coach's meeting. If it wasn't for the guy I loved living in it, I would never have stepped inside. It wasn't flat-out filthy, but it was close, and the whole place—no matter if it was morning or afternoon, weekend or weekday—smelled like dirty laundry and sex.

"I'll walk you in," he said, still shirtless, still smiling. Having to sit next to Jude for the whole car ride, and keep-ing my hands off him, should have earned me some sort of medal in restraint. A big one.

"You've got a game to win," I said, kissing the corner of his mouth that was upturned. "I know my way around."

"Watch your step. I think Ben might have had a party last

night while the rest of us were gone, and you know how his parties are," he said, catching my chin between his thumb and finger. He moved closer, and his lips barely grazed mine before they ended on the underside of my jaw. Running his lips down, his teeth grazed the sensitive skin. And he was still shirtless, so I could see every muscle that tightened and rolled as his mouth explored my neck.

Screw the medal, I deserved sainthood.

I trembled when his mouth left me. Unmistakably trembled, like I was experiencing withdrawal.

I knew he'd be gloating. Jude loved the way he could make me feel. But I was starting to get a little tired of all the foreplay leading up to a whole lotta nothing.

Reaching for the door handle, I exhaled, working to compose myself. "See you in a few," I said. "I'll be one of fifty thousand screaming, throwing my arms in the air, and yelling your name."

"You're the only thing I see out there, Luce," he said as I scooted out of the door.

He handed me my bag, propping his other arm over the steering wheel. I wanted to take a picture to freeze that moment. It would keep me warm during the cold winter nights in New York when I slept solo in my bed.

"Yeah, you're kind of the only thing I see out there too,"

I teased. "But it's mainly because of the way your butt looks in that spandex."

He huffed. "And I thought I was the world champ in objectification."

"*Was*, Ryder," I clarified, "*was* being the operative word."

FOUR

At least the shower Jude and Tony shared was clean. Clean by college-boy standards.

It had taken a half hour of scalding hot water to fully warm me back up. I couldn't remember a shower ever feeling so good, especially knowing it was where Jude stood naked at least once a day. I closed my eyes, imagining him, as I soaped my body with his bath wash.

Winding my hair into a towel, I brushed my teeth and slipped into my jeans and Jude's favorite Syracuse football sweatshirt. It still smelled like him. Fortunately, his good smell—soap and man—and not the way he smelled post-practice.

I slipped on my boots before leaving the bathroom because Jude hadn't exaggerated—his bedroom was a mess. Like someone-might-want-to-consider-calling-the-hazmat-team kind of a mess. I'd had to dodge obstacles like beer bottles, cardboard cutouts of bikini-clad women lying on the floor sideways, and a few pairs of crumpled-up boxers to get to Jude's room earlier. The only thing that made his room cleaner than the rest of the house was the lack of girly cardboard cutouts decorating the floor.

Closing the bathroom door behind me, I stepped back into Jude's room, stopping in my tracks almost immediately. This was not the same room I'd left thirty minutes ago. I had to double-check for the photo of the two of us on his dresser to assure myself this was, in fact, Jude's room.

The room was clean, almost sparkling clean. The bed was made; the corners had even been pulled tight and folded over. There wasn't a single article of clothing decorating the carpet or any other flat surface.

Walking tentatively across a room I didn't recognize, I slid open the top drawer of my dresser and shoved my toiletry bag back inside. Jude and I tried to switch weekends—when he wasn't at away games. Instead of just lending me a drawer for my stuff, he'd gone out and bought a whole dresser just for my use. The gesture had left me speechless.

Sliding the drawer closed, I took another look at the room. The picture of us caught my attention again. Taking a few steps closer, I saw why. A fine line ran diagonally across the glass, cutting between Jude and me almost perfectly.

Lifting the picture, I ran my finger along the crack, suppressing a shudder.

"Sorry about that."

I startled, the picture slipping from my hands and careening into the corner of Jude's nightstand. The glass shattered one more time, but didn't break completely.

Sure I'd cry if I continued to stare at the fractured photo at my feet, I spun around. Bad move.

"I accidentally knocked it over earlier when I was cleaning." A tall, lean girl in an orange-and-white cheer uniform scurried around Jude's room, not looking at me.

"Who are you?" I asked, crossing my arms. But I already knew.

"Adriana," she said, offering nothing else as she carried an overflowing laundry basket of folded clothes over to Jude's dresser. "You know, no one's allowed in a player's room pregame except for his Spirit Sister," she said, pulling open the top drawer before she began stacking Jude's underwear inside.

Two emotions hit me right then, watching Adriana Vix—a girl who was all legs and boobs—pawing all over my boyfriend's clean underwear. There was anger—pure and raw—like the kind Jude felt. And there was something else that clenched my throat and heart tight, feeling like both might break.

"I'm his girlfriend," I replied, trying not to let the anger show. "I'm allowed anytime I want. You can run that by Jude if you don't believe me. And what the hell is a Spirit Sister? Other than the obvious," I finished, looking her up and down before wrinkling my nose.

She was bronzed, dark-haired, and had these grassy green eyes that almost glowed against her dark skin. Her legs were so long her cheer skirt appeared more like a pair of panties than a skirt, and as Tony had so ardently put it, she had huge boobs. And apparently had no problem letting the world know it on a leave-nothing-to-the-imagination scale.

"Each one of the cheerleaders is assigned to one of the football players. One of the top-performing football players, because there aren't enough of us to cover them all, and what's the point of waiting hand and foot on the benchers anyways?" she explained, sliding Jude's top drawer closed and moving to the second one. Folded and pressed shirts went into that one, color coded. Of course.

"I'm the captain of my team, and Jude's the star of his. We're an obvious match," she said, smiling into Jude's clean shirts.

It was almost impressive how compelled I felt to rip out clumps of this chick's shiny dark hair. I knew there'd be consequences, possibly even an overnighter in prison. And I didn't care.

"Obvious," I deadpanned, narrowing my eyes as she moved to the next drawer, stacking three of the four pairs of pants Jude owned. "So what? As Spirit Sisters you get to clean their rooms, do their laundry, bake them brownies, that kind of fifties housewife shit?" Ah, there it was. That temper I needed so I didn't choke on my words in front of exotic Cheerleader Barbie.

Turning around, she dropped the empty laundry basket on the floor. "And whatever other needs they might have," she said, her conniving smile telling the whole story.

I felt my fists balling, bracing for impact. I'd never been in a catfight, but I felt that might change . . . soon.

"Listen, Adriana, wasn't it?" I said, coming around to the foot of Jude's bed, standing as tall as I could. She still towered a solid half foot above me. "I know the game you're playing. I've seen it played a million different times and a million different ways. But let me save you the time and energy and just let you know how this ends."

I took another step forward, crossing my arms because I didn't trust them not to act on their own and land a punch right between those intense green eyes. "You will lose. Jude's with me and I'm with Jude. The end. You can ask him if you need further explanation."

Adriana's lips pursed for a moment before they flattened back into that fake smile. "You don't do his laundry, you don't clean his room, and I can tell just by looking at you that you don't put out, so what good are you to him? A guy has needs. He might be yours today. But what about tomorrow?" She leaned into his dresser, her fingers playing with the corner of it. I didn't want her fingers on anything of Jude's. Ever.

"All right, let me put this in a way you'll understand," I said, steepling my fingers under my chin. "Stay away from Jude or I will, figuratively and literally, kick your ass. With a smile," I added, plastering one on.

Arching her meticulously sculpted eyebrows, Adriana clucked her tongue. "You want to know what happened to the last girl who stood in my way?"

Not really. But I couldn't resist. "What?"

She lifted a shoulder, bounding across the room toward the door on those never-ending legs. "Who knows? I never heard anything about her again after I landed her man," she said, eyeing me. "She was drowned in my wake. You better hope you can swim if you go up against me."

This bitch was lucky I was letting her leave in one piece. "Like a damn fish."

By the time I'd weaved my way through thousands of 'Cuse fans to get to my reserved home-game seat, my anger and hatred for Adriana hadn't lessened one bit. Miss Vix and I were a catfight waiting to happen.

Sidestepping along the front row, carefully balancing my popcorn and hot chocolate in my arms, I was surprised to see a familiar face in the seat next to mine—front and center.

"Hey, you!" Holly shouted at me above the roar of the crowd, grabbing the popcorn so I could get myself situated.

"I didn't think you could make it," I replied, giving her a sideways hug before sitting down. Syracuse had yet to take the field, but we were seconds away. Good thing, too. Jude leading his team out on the field to the adoration of thousands, that spandex highlighting those muscles of his . . . well, it was a sight I never wanted to miss.

Keeping my eyes locked on the tunnel that led from the locker room to the field, I nudged Holly's leg. "Your mom agreed to watch little Jude for a night?"

"It took some convincing, and I had to agree to frost her hair free of charge for a year, but yeah, she agreed. I also had to perm, like, a dozen heads of old-lady hair at the nursing home in town to pay for the airfare," Holly said, tossing a piece of popcorn into her mouth. "This is my first night off, and judging by Mom's lack of enthusiasm for watching her only grandchild, it will probably be my last for a while. So I'm letting my hair down tonight, girl." Weaving her fingers through her hair, Holly mussed it, then threw her head forward, giving it a shake. "Fair warning," she added, when she swung her head back up. Her long blond hair had just achieved an inch and a half of added volume.

I laughed, holding out my hot cocoa. She took it, shooting a smile my way.

After learning she wasn't Jude's baby mama, I was able to appreciate Holly in a new way—sans jealousy. And I'd grown to like her. A lot. Our looks weren't our only similarity—our personalities were so in line she could often finish my sentences, and vice versa.

The visiting team came out of their tunnel, welcomed by the booing of almost the whole dome. Holly joined in, lobbing a few pieces of popcorn onto the field.

And then the flags of orange and white, followed by a backflipping, high-kicking cheer crew I now hated based on principle, burst out of the home team tunnel. I didn't need to check the number on his chest to locate Jude when he sprinted out behind the cheerleaders. He had a particular swagger, even in a run, that I'd be able to identify fifty years from now.

"I swear he swaggers in his sleep," I yelled over at Holly.

"Yeah, but Jude's swagger is justified. He struts because

he's confident in his . . . *talent*," she said, tipping the hot cocoa cup to her lips.

"You said it," I mumbled, but it was lost in the sea of noise.

The stadium went nuts, screaming, chanting, and bowing as their hero led his team onto the field. In barely two months of college play, Jude had become somewhat of a legend. He played on a whole different level than the rest of the college boys. He played like he was a football god. And his fans worshipped him that way.

Jumping up in my seat and dragging Holly up with me, I bounced and cheered with the best of them. So much that I was hoarse when Jude took his spot on the sidelines, right in my line of sight. The coach was talking to him, but Jude looked back, his eyes finding me right away. The benefits of reserving the front-and-center seat for your girlfriend. He waved at Holly, then winked at me, which I answered with an air kiss. His grin showed through the slats in his helmet before he turned his attention back to his coach.

"That boy has such a stare-worthy, needs-to-be-grabbed-in-handfuls ass," Holly said, gazing a little dreamily at Jude's backside. I would have been jealous had it been anyone else. Holly, Jude's childhood best friend—and only Holly—could make a blunt comment about Jude's ass without me going all territorial girlfriend on her. She'd known him forever. She had earned the right.

"I mean, that's something a girl could hold on to in bed," Holly added, munching on a piece of popcorn.

Heat rushed my cheeks as I visualized what she was saying.

Like he could feel our eyes on him, Jude shifted his arm behind him and gave his own butt a smack, throwing me a quick smirk over his shoulder before huddling up with a few of his starters.

Cruel.

"So," Holly began, elbowing at my side, "you guys . . . ?"

I glared at her.

"That's a *no*," she said, halfway hiding her smile behind the hot chocolate.

I watched as Jude and the guys took the field after the kickoff. Number twenty-three's jersey caught my attention. HOPKINS now said DOUCHE in black Sharpie on a piece of duct tape. Jude took payback seriously.

"Well, it hasn't been for lack of trying," I said, turning in my seat to face Holly. One of Holly's best traits? She wasn't judgmental. I could tell her anything. I bet she wouldn't flinch if I divulged I had some sort of toe-sucking fetish. "On my part, at least," I added.

"You know it isn't because he doesn't want to, right?" she said, looking over at me. "Because he wants you so bad he's about to explode. He's just hell-bent on doing this whole thing 'right.' He doesn't want to screw anything up. You know he believes screwing up is in his nature." She paused as Jude lined up behind his offensive line. I hopped up with the rest of the fans. "Just give him some time."

"If it takes much more time, I'm going to shrivel up and die, and then whether it's right or wrong to sleep with me won't matter," I responded, crossing my fingers as Jude crouched into position.

"Girl, I know the feeling," Holly said. "I rode around the block a number of times *before* little Jude."

"God, Holly," I said, almost choking on a kernel of popcorn. The center hiked the ball and I froze. Jude faked to one side, then the other, arching the football back in his hand as Tony charged down the field. Jude's arm blurred, the ball flying into a praiseworthy spiral, ticking off the yards until it landed in Tony's cradled arms at the fifteen.

The crowd exploded, pom-poms shaking, foam hands bouncing, rabid fans chanting.

"Damn!" Holly shouted over at me. "Our boy isn't just out there for eye candy, huh?"

"He can play," I said. "Eye candy is just a little something extra on the side."

Holly said something back, but Jude was in position again, and I tuned everything else out. This time, as soon as he caught the ball, he ran it. Dodging a couple of players who slipped by his line, he blazed a path past the ten, past the five, and then the last few yards were wide open.

And we were on the scoreboard with six points, less than a minute into the game. I knew there was no *J* in team, but this was almost all thanks to number seventeen, Jude Ryder.

I jumped in place, screaming out at the field. Holly was screaming too, although her shouts were punctuated by "fine ass" and "eye candy."

Jude dropped the ball in the end zone. After single-handedly turning around Southpointe High's notorious losing streak, he'd abandoned his post-touchdown theatrics in college.

But there was one opening touchdown tradition he hadn't let die. I was already leaning over the railing before he'd jogged over the ten. It felt like half the dome's eyes were on me, because even fans who had been to just one game knew why Jude Ryder was sliding his helmet off and who his smile was for—me.

I'd never been one for big PDAs, but when it came to Jude, I'd take him any way, anytime. No matter if we were alone or in front of thousands of crazed fans. When we were looking at each other like this, everything else faded into oblivion.

Shouldering a path through his teammates, who slapped

him on the back as he passed, he dropped his helmet before leaping into the air. His hands caught the top railing of the front row as he lifted himself up.

Leaning over farther, I grinned down at his sweaty face. "Show-off," I whispered, so close I could almost taste the salt on his skin.

His smile brightened. "Come here," he mock-ordered, dropping his gaze to my lips.

I tasted the salty sweat of his skin as I kissed him. The crowd's roar increased tenfold, loving the show their star quarterback was giving them. But we weren't doing it for them. This, we did for us.

He didn't let me break away when I shifted. Instead, he somehow managed to hold himself with one arm while the other grabbed the back of my neck and pulled me closer toward him. He kissed me harder, until the stadium started spinning out of the corner of my eyes.

Then, leaning back, he pressed one last sweet kiss into my lips. "My God, Luce," he murmured, the warmth of his breath coating my face, "how's a guy supposed to play football after that?"

"Good luck with that," I answered, my voice teasing.

"There better be more where that came from after the game," he said, flashing an impish grin as he lowered himself onto the field.

"Plenty."

"Ryder!" the head coach hollered above the noise. "I sure as hell know you don't mind making a fool of yourself, but quit making fools of me and the rest of the team! Calm your dick down and focus!"

Jude rolled his eyes up at me before turning and heading back to the sideline.

"Good to see you too, Jude!" Holly yelled, crossing her arms and looking playfully put out.

Spinning around, Jude extended his arms. "You know I love ya, Hol!"

"Yeah, yeah," she muttered, waving him off.

And then Cheerleader Barbie put herself in Jude's path, hands on her hips, and gave him a look that made me see red all over again. She said something, but I couldn't hear her. I knew that if I were a lip reader, I would have been throwing myself over the railing and slapping that suggestive little smile right off her face.

Jude nodded in acknowledgment, reaching down to retrieve his helmet. Adriana moved faster, grabbing the helmet and swinging it out of his grasp. Jude reached for it, but she dodged him, lifting it higher. Jude's expression wasn't amused. Mine had gone from unamused straight to enraged. This girl was resorting to playground tactics to get his attention. It was weak. And pathetic. I'd seen her before at the games, flirting with Jude like all the girls did, but now she was pulling out the big guns.

Adriana sidestepped, dangling the helmet just past Jude's fingertips. He paused, putting his hands on his hips, and blew out a breath. It kind of looked like he said *please*, to which she shook her head. Then her eyes landed on me before she tapped the side of her face with one claw—I mean, finger. She waited, making sure I was watching. Damn right, I was watching.

So when Jude leaned in and gave her a peck on the cheek, she got to see me turning a shade of purple I know I turned. Lowering the helmet, she handed it back to him, but not before she lifted an eyebrow at me and settled a victorious smile into place.

"Who is that bitch?" Holly said, sounding as furious as I felt.

I glowered a hole through her back as Adriana spun around and rejoined the rest of her Spirit Sisters. I planned my revenge. "Cheerleader Barbie," I seethed. "About to be Dead Barbie."

FIVE

"*P*ut this on," Holly ordered me, throwing a wad of red cloth my way. Catching it before it parachuted over my face, I held it in front of me. It was a strapless, slinky, knee-length dress.

"Why?" I asked. To most of the male population, this was considered hot. In my world, it was considered trashy.

"Because you're going to beat that Vix bitch at her own game," she sneered, unfolding a white halter dress that was way shorter than the one she had just tossed at me.

"Vix bitch," I repeated as I slid Jude's sweatshirt over my head. "Catchy."

"That's because her ancestors were the inspiration for the term."

I chuckled as I peeled my skinny jeans off, glad Holly was there. She'd all but held my hand through the rest of the game (which 'Cuse won, thanks to a certain quarterback getting a total of seven passes into the end zone). Between blistering holes into Adriana's back and screaming at the top of my lungs after every completed pass, I was totally drained. And kind of a wreck.

"What time is it?" I asked as Holly texted someone.

"About time you get your ass in that dress and show Vix bitch that revenge is a dish best served with a smokin' side of Lucy."

I sighed.

"Just hurry, okay? The street's already packed with cars, and the team's going to be rolling up soon. You want to be down there when Jude struts in, because you're going to be the only thing he sees," Holly said, shuffling out of her own clothes and sliding into the white dress.

It was a team tradition for Jude's house to host the home game after-parties. There was never a lack of women or alcohol, and inhibitions were always in short supply, so a wild time was a sure thing to be had. During the last party, Jude and I hid out in his dark room, petting the hell out of each other. I would be more than okay with a repeat performance tonight.

Tying the halter behind her neck, Holly began sifting through her makeup bag. Grabbing a few tubes, she started toward me, wielding them like weapons.

"Hold still," she ordered, uncapping smoky black eyeliner.

"Make me," I shot back, knowing arguing with Holly was useless.

"Don't think I won't."

Giving in, I closed my eyes and let her have her way. The girl lined, mascaraed, and glossed me in under a minute. She had a gift.

"What size shoe do you wear?" she asked, hurrying back over to her suitcase while I smacked my lips together.

"Seven and a half."

"Perfect." Wrenching a pair of black patent-leather pumps from her bag, she dropped them on the floor.

I tried sliding my foot inside one—not happening. A quick look at the size confirmed why. "These are sixes," I said, wondering which would be better—my boots or going barefoot.

"So?" she said, dabbing her lips with pink gloss.

How was I not making sense? "So . . . that's one and a half sizes too small." Duh.

"Pain is beauty, sweetlips," she said, extracting a pair of silver strappy heels from the duffel and fastening them on. "Put those sexy-ass shoes on and work it."

"Why argue?" I asked, wincing as I worked my right foot into the tiny shoe, praying a few hours of wearing them tonight wouldn't affect my dancing for the next few weeks.

"You could," she said, throwing her head forward and teasing her roots. "But it would be a waste of time."

"I figured," I muttered, bracing myself as I slid my other foot into its torture device.

"Okay, let me get a look at you," she said, sliding an earring on. She studied me, like a painter would contemplate her masterpiece, and a slow smile spread across her face. "Take off your underwear."

"What?" I was never prepared for what came out of Holly's mouth. "No!"

"Take. Them. Off," she repeated.

"You take yours off," I threw back, aware that I sounded like a child.

Her smile broadened. "They already are, baby."

Shudder. Too much information.

"Holly," I said, "I'm not taking my underwear off. End of story."

"Oh yes, you are," she fired back. "End of story."

I opened my mouth, but nothing came out. I wasn't sure a logical argument would work against her insanity.

"Lucy, if you want to rub Adriana Vix's perfect little face in her own pile of shit, you've got to have as many tricks in your bag as she does. I know her type, and they play dirty. And they're relentless little ho-bags."

She stomped over to me, fists on her hips. "Trick number one: your hot little number dress," she started, waving her hands down my body. "Trick number two: You're going to give Jude a pair of heavy-lidded bedroom eyes anytime he looks your way. Trick number three: You'll act gracious and flattered when the guys line up around you. It will drive him nuts." Holly must not know Jude as well as she thought if she was crazy enough to think any guy within the whole state would make a pass at me with him in the same room. "And trick number four"—she wagged her brows at me suggestively—"if Adriana comes within an arm's length of him, you discreetly slip your panties into his hand and walk away."

For a certifiable loon, she made a lot of sense.

Holly waited while I worked all this out in my head. Finally, I accepted that any plan was better than no plan. I hitched my dress up and worked my underwear down my legs. Thank *someone* up there I'd worn a lacy pair that would definitely drive Jude up the wall.

Balling them up, I held my fist in front of her. "And where am I supposed to keep these while I'm waiting for the perfect time to slip them into his hand?"

See, she hadn't thought of everything.

Rolling her eyes, she grabbed them from me and stuffed them between my cleavage.

"There," she said, patting my boobs. "You're good to go."

"*So* happy you're here, Holly," I said, combing my fingers through my hair and trying the flip-and-tease thing she did so often. "To make me paranoid I'm about to lose my boyfriend to Adriana Vix."

"That's not what I'm saying, Lucy Larson," she said, looking offended. "I know how Jude feels about you. That kind of crazy love runs deep, babe. He's not going anywhere." Opening Jude's door, she motioned me out. "It's not him I'm worried about. It's that Vix bitch. That breed of woman has made an art form out of manipulating men before they even know what hit them. They're dangerous, so the sooner you show her she's not getting her claws into your guy, the sooner she can move on to the next couple she wants to tear apart."

I took a deep breath. "All right, let's do this."

"Thatta girl," she said, smacking my butt as I passed her. "Time to rock 'n' roll."

The music started pumping as we strode down the hall—some thumping hip-hop that made the floor vibrate.

"I know you've got a streak of diva in you, Lucy," Holly said as we rounded the corner to the stairs. "But tonight, I need you to set that diva free. Got it?"

"Got it," I said, surveying the living room, which was

already past max capacity—and the football team wasn't even here yet.

Winding our way through the crush of bodies, I saw that Holly's impromptu makeover had the desired effect. Every male within a ten-foot radius turned to watch us slide by.

"Hey, asshole!" Holly hollered behind me. "Keep your hands to yourself unless you want me to chop them off while you sleep!"

The offender raised his hands and backed away.

So maybe it had been a little *too* effective.

"This is good!" she shouted above the music, stopping short. "The first thing Jude will see is you when he comes through the door."

"You really have all the bases covered," I said, telling myself the guy beside me wasn't purposely brushing up against me.

"Location, location, location," she quoted, smoothing my dress down before lifting my boobs higher.

The mouth of the guy behind Holly dropped.

"Stop," I demanded, shooing her hands away.

"Fine," she said, giving them one final pop. "Just remember. The diva to end all divas."

I nodded. *Diva, diva, diva. Think like a diva; act like a diva. Diva is a state of mind.* My mental mantras weren't helping, so

I decided to put some of Holly's theory into practice.

Turning to the guy still pretending he wasn't grinding up on me, I worked a half smile into place and looked up at him through my lashes. "Sure is hot in here," I said slowly, with a slight drawl.

Grinder Boy's eyes widened; I could almost see the pulse quicken in his neck. "It sure is," he replied, moving closer and resting a hand on my side.

"I could sure use something to cool off." I ran my right hand up and down my left arm, like I was soothing my nonexistent goose bumps. His eyes appeared torn between watching my fingers caress my skin and staring at my cleavage.

Wetting his lips, he leaned in closer. Close enough to know I'd . . . *ahem*, hit my mark.

"I think I'm up to the challenge," he said, his mouth curving up at both ends.

"Hey, Mr. Overeager." Holly stepped in. "She means a drink. A *cold* drink."

Shaking his head, he cleared his throat and stepped back. "Oh yeah," he said. "Sure. I'm on it." Casting one longing look my way, he started tearing through the crowd, headed for the kitchen.

"You know not to drink anything he gives you, right?"

Holly said as we watched him embark on his one-man crusade.

"Obviously," I replied. "How was that for diva?"

"You're a natural," she said, nudging me. "Keep up the good work."

The music came to an abrupt halt, a few beats of silence filling the room before the first notes of "Eye of the Tiger" blared through the speakers. All hail the victors—the team had arrived. If the song didn't give them away, the chanting that had started outside did the job.

"Showtime," Holly said, elbowing me.

"Will you stop throwing elbows?" I hissed over at her. "I'm going to look like a purple Dalmatian by the time you leave tomorrow."

"Oh, grow a pair," she muttered, focusing on the front door. "Diva," she added.

"Brat."

"Ooh. Burn," she deadpanned, elbowing at me again.

This time, I dodged her bony little elbow.

The kicker, Kurt or Kirk, was the first through the door, one of the cheerleaders—no doubt his Spirit Sister—hanging off his arm. Right behind the K-named kicker, Tony came in, a petite blonde bouncing beside him.

The players had never arrived like this before; Jude

usually just came barreling through the door first, yelling some obscenity, before making a beeline for me and finding a quiet spot where we could be alone.

I knew exactly who and what was responsible for the change. The *who* being Adriana Vix. And the *what* being her nasty plan to throw me out with the trash.

"All right, Lucy, get into position," Holly said, shuffling me right by the door. "This chick's coming out of the gates swinging."

"No shit," I said, shaking my head as the parade continued. I wasn't holding my breath for Jude anytime soon; I knew she was saving their entrance for the grand finale.

"Here, lean your hip on this," Holly instructed, pushing me sideways until I bumped into an old, water-damaged sofa table. Standing in front of me, she positioned my hip where she wanted it, then grabbed my hand. "Hand on hip, feet crossed at the ankles." Her gaze met mine with a hardened degree of seriousness. "When he walks in and his eyes fall on you, I want your eyes to look all innocent. And I want your mouth to open just a bit—like during orgasm. Got it?"

"Sure?" I answered, because there wasn't any time for clarification. I could see the top of Jude's head coming up the front stairs. A shiny dark-haired head bobbed a few inches below it.

"Put a nail in her casket," Holly said, driving her fist into her hand before disappearing into the crowd.

Though he was partially obscured by a mass of bodies, as Jude moved into the room, my pulse kicked up. Even with that *thing* glued to his arm, the sight of him made my legs weaken.

As expected, Adriana was beaming like she was walking across the Miss America stage. Seriously, I was going to make her cry if she didn't loosen her grip on Jude's forearm. Strutting into the room like she was the main attraction, she waved at the crowd. She was wearing a simple, short, turquoise dress that made her skin glow in its bronzeness.

The crowd was chanting, "Ry-der, Ry-der, Ry-der," and my heart was beating two beats a syllable. He'd changed from his uniform to a snug-fitting white V-neck tee and dark jeans that hung off his hips, finished off with his worn pair of Cons.

We had been together over a year, on and off, and he could still make me swoon just by looking at him. What this guy saw in me, I still hadn't figured out, but my plan was to fake-it-till-I-make-it. I hoped that one day, I'd become the girl Jude deserved.

As Jude and Adriana blazed through the crowd, it began to part, opening up to where I leaned against the beat-up table, hand on hip, eyes and mouth ready to carry out their orders. Holly couldn't have placed me in a better location.

Adriana saw me first, and her face screwed into a smirk as her hand curled deeper into Jude's muscles.

But I didn't deviate from the plan—resisting the urge to slap her—and my willpower paid off. Jude's gaze didn't only shift to me. He stopped in his tracks; he didn't even blink. "Wow," he mouthed at me, running his eyes up and down my body.

Opening my eyes wider, I blinked slowly, projecting as much innocence as I was capable of. Then, biting my lower lip suggestively, I parted my mouth just so, hopefully making Holly proud.

Jude might have stumbled in place. Adriana's scowl deepened.

I owed Holly. Big-time.

Wrestling out of Adriana's death grip, he cut across the room toward me. Adriana slammed her hands on her hips, looking one second away from exploding. Beautiful.

Even more beautiful was the guy grinning at me as he shoved through the rest of the crowd, moving as fast as he could. When he reached me, his eyes were as big as Bambi's.

"Damn, Luce," he said, sounding out of breath, checking me out again with the excitement and anticipation of unwrapping a present.

I didn't have any words for him. Flattening my hands

over his shoulders, I pressed against him. His mouth parted with surprise. The heels made it so I didn't have to press onto my tiptoes when I crushed my mouth into his like all we had left in life was this moment.

One stunned moment later, his hands lowered into place over my hips, gripping them with an urgency that tightened the muscles in my thighs. The crowd had starting whistling at our *very* public display of affection, and when Jude's hand crept over and around a few inches, digging into the flesh of my butt, they started whooping.

I ran my hands up his neck to cradle his face. I looked up into those hungry eyes, feeling the warmth of his breath over me.

"Good game."

SIX

"**Y**ou better not be staring at what I think you are, Kurt," Jude warned, reappearing with a couple of beers in hand and clearing up the mystery of the kicker's name once and for all.

"No way," Kurt said, tilting his beer at me before fading into the crowd.

"Yes way," Jude muttered, handing me one of the beers before resting his hand on my side. "Not that I can blame him."

Clanking my bottle against Jude's, I took a swallow. "But you'll kick his ass if he does it again?" I guessed.

"Hell yeah I will," he said, nuzzling my neck before he laid a path of kisses down it. The slippery glass bottle almost fell from my hands. "That goes for you too, Denoza," Jude said, peering over at one of his teammates next to us while his mouth continued to wet the skin above my collarbone. "And I'll start by prying out those wandering eyes."

"Sorry, Ryder. Sorry, Lucy," Denoza said, sheepishly. "What can I say? Your girl is meant to be stared at."

"That's right. She is," Jude said, blocking off Denoza completely. "By me."

Denoza lifted his hands in surrender. "No harm, no foul, man," he said before setting his sights on a girl sprawled out on the stairs.

"Not in my book," Jude muttered after him, before turning around. "You're gonna get me killed, Luce," he said, his mouth twisting when he took another look at me. "I'm a tough son of a bitch, and I can fight off every one of these guys one loser at a time, but I think they could take me if they all came at me at once."

"Should I go change?" I suggested, taking a step toward the stairs.

"Shit, no," Jude said, grabbing my hand and pulling me back. "I just wish it was a party of two so I could enjoy you all to myself."

Lifting my arms, I wound them over his neck and started swaying in time to our own beat.

"It *is* just you and me, baby," I said, resting my head against his chest, closing my eyes when his arms fastened around me. The music wasn't right, the crowd wasn't right, but everything about the way Jude held me was perfect.

Not even a minute later, the music came to a screeching halt. Jude and I continued to sway in the silence.

"Okay, everyone," a familiar voice cooed through a microphone. "It's time to play a new after-party game that's *sure* to become a favorite."

I thought we'd been playing a game all night.

Sighing, I lifted my head from Jude's chest to see what the bitch had up her sleeve now.

"As everyone knows, the starters are all assigned a Spirit Sister at the beginning of the year." I rolled my eyes as her posse grouped around Adriana, cheering her on. "Our goal is to make their lives easier so they can focus on kicking ass every Saturday!"

A roar burst through the room.

"But a boy's got to have his fun too, right?" Adriana's brows lifted suggestively as the noise rose to a deafening level.

"So tonight marks the beginning of a new Spirit Sister tradition." Extending the arm she'd hidden behind her back, she revealed a full bottle of vodka. Another explosion of cheering. Over a pretty girl holding a bottle of liquor.

Pretty depressing.

"We don't just do your laundry and make you brownies, we'll get you drunk as a skunk, too!" Adriana waited for the crowd to quiet before continuing. I felt sick to my stomach even before her eyes landed on Jude. Which they did. "Each Spirit Sister will serve a shot to her assigned player, starting with the quarterback."

Yep, that's what I was waiting for. She was using this flimsy excuse of a game and "team spirit" to separate Jude and me. Holly was unfortunately on target with her "tricks up her sleeve" predictions.

"That means you, Jude Ryder!" Adriana shouted into the microphone, waving the bottle at him.

Jude groaned and looked over at me. But before he could say anything, a herd of his teammates began pushing him toward the front of the room.

"Don't worry, Jude's date for the night, you'll get him back," Adriana said, smiling maliciously at me. I wanted to slap that smug smile off her face. Slick move, referring to me as nothing more than "Jude's date." "That is, if he *wants* to come back after playing our game."

A couple of guys nearby hung their heads back and made catcalls and wolf whistles. Taylor had been right all along; men really had evolved from apes.

Pushing Jude up next to Adriana, the herders stepped back into the crowd so everyone could see what was happening in the spotlight. I didn't like how Jude was standing so close to Adriana, seeing how close in height they were.

They'd fit together perfectly. Why my mind went there, I don't know, but the image of Jude bracing himself above Adriana while he kissed her made me want to hurl.

"Here's how this works," Adriana said, addressing Jude, who was rubbing the back of his neck, looking deep in deer-in-the-headlights mode. "Shot glass," she began, lifting a small glass. "Shot," she continued, pouring the clear liquid to the brim. Then, handing the bottle off to one of her fellow cheerleaders, she raised her index finger to the crowd, who were looking around at each other like *big deal*.

Inching down the top of her dress, she tucked the shot glass deep in her craterlike cleavage. "Enjoy," she instructed. "No hands allowed."

Hell no.

The rest of the guys had turned into one connected being, throwing their arms in the air and cheering in unison.

Adriana ate it up, managing a tiny curtsy without spilling a drop, right before her gaze shifted to me. "What are you waiting for, Jude?" she said, looking right into my narrowed eyes. "Drink up."

"What are you doing standing here, you stupid, stupid girl?" Holly hissed beside me, shoving me toward the front of the room. Reaching down my dress for a quick second, she then slapped the panties into my hand. "Go beat that bitch at her own game."

It took one more solid shove from Holly, but then I shook out of my stupor and charged forward. Pushing through the bodies chanting "Ry-der" and throwing fist pumps into the air, I balled the panties up into my hand, watching Jude, who was watching me. I had his attention, probably because he was worried about me getting eye molested by one of his teammates. Right now, I'd take his attention any way I could get it.

"Your shot's getting warm," Adriana said into the microphone, giving her chest a little shake. This time, a splash of liquid spilled out, running down her dress.

Squeezing by the last hulk of a man standing between me and Jude, I brushed past my star quarterback. I curled my pinkie over his, waiting for his hand to open. As soon as it did, I slipped the lacy thong into his hands, arched a brow at him, and kept on going.

I walked away from Jude, who was standing next to Adriana, as his team and the entire room waited for him to liberate a shot of vodka from Tits "R" Us. I was in hyperventilation mode. But I couldn't turn back. I had to trust in Holly's man-eater wisdom. I prayed that she knew what she was doing.

The crowd thinned a little by the hallway, and there were barely any party stragglers when I walked into the bathroom at the end of it. Closing the door behind me, I braced my hands over the sink and focused on breathing.

Before I'd taken one complete breath, the door creaked open. I looked up in the mirror, a smile splitting my face when I saw Jude's bewildered expression staring back at me.

"I think you lost something," he said in a low voice, lifting his hand and letting my underwear dangle from his finger.

My smile stretched further until it actually hurt. "Looks like the right person found it."

Stepping inside, Jude shut the door behind him. The bathroom was small, and that was being generous. With the two of us crammed inside, my butt was halfway propped on the sink counter and Jude's back was pressed up against the shower door.

"So does this mean . . . ?" he said, gazing down my body, ending at my hips. I felt every muscle inside of me contract, then go soft.

"Why don't you find out for yourself?" I whispered, my breath already coming in short bursts.

His eyes stayed fixed just south of my navel as a slow smile crept into place. "Happily," he said, his voice husky and deep.

Jude threw himself against me, lifting me onto the counter at the same time. His mouth covered mine, forcing his tongue inside and running it every which way. I was so overwhelmed, my head knocked the mirror as I tried to keep pace with him.

Right in the middle of our kiss, Jude pulled back suddenly, appraising me where I sat on the counter, heaving like I'd run a two-minute mile. Looking down at the sliver of space between my legs, his forehead creased like he was trying to answer the world's most complicated question. Grabbing my waist, he scooted me down to the very edge of the counter. Placing his hand on the inside of one knee, he pushed it to the side. Doing the same with the other knee, he stepped between my legs.

Gripping the hem of my dress with both hands, Jude rolled it up slowly, his thumbs trailing along the sensitive skin of my inner thighs. My heart was racing.

And he hadn't even touched me *there* yet.

His fingers rolled the dress higher, and then higher still. The entire journey up, Jude's eyes stayed fixed on mine. Like he wanted to see every reaction on my face as he touched me.

One more roll and the dress was at my belly button. My body was aching for a release, pulsing more intensely than it ever had.

Jude's thumb skimmed up the rest of my inner thigh. When he pulled it away, I almost whimpered out loud. And then, when he lowered it back a few inches higher, where the throbbing was the worst, I did cry out. Grabbing the edges of the counter, I forced myself to keep looking into his darkening eyes.

"Damn," he breathed, all throaty and rough.

I couldn't speak—I was one stroke past words.

Closing the space between us, he kissed the corner of my mouth. "I love you," he whispered outside my ear, right before his thumb started moving again in slow circles.

My head fell back, smashing into the mirror once more, but the dull pain felt good paired with the acute pressure spreading its way through my body in waves.

My breath came in shorter gasps as everything tightened. I was so close.

"I love you so damn much, Luce," Jude said in between kisses. Now his mouth was exploring my throat.

And that was all I needed. My fingers dug into his back as my body quaked against his.

As my muscles went limp, I let myself curl into him even more. I managed to sigh through my staggered breathing. I could feel his smile against my skin.

Holy shit. I knew my body was still intact, but a few moments ago it felt like it was falling apart from the center. I couldn't calm my breathing, and my legs were still trembling as Jude continued sucking on my smooth shoulder.

Right as my head was falling back again, the bathroom

door burst open, slamming into Jude.

"Oops. I think we better find you another bathroom." Holly peered over Adriana's shoulder, shooting me a quick conspirator's smile. Adriana took in the scene, me on the counter, my legs wrapped around him, Jude trailing kisses across my skin with his mouth. Tears—not her first tonight, apparently—welled up in her reddened eyes. "This one's . . . *occupied*," Holly added, winking at me before pulling on Adriana's elbow.

But before Adriana backed out of the room, her eyes met mine. My mouth curved up, my lips still parted from my clipped breathing. Keeping her gaze, I curled my fingers into Jude's back, arching my neck higher to give him better access. I didn't have to utter a single word for Adriana to get the message. It was crystal clear.

Jude was mine.

Only after the door closed again did Jude's mouth slow. Giving one last nip over my shoulder blade, he lifted his head. His face was smug and happy as he assessed the effect he'd had on me.

"I guess she figured out what 'came up' when I left her high and dry with a shot between her tits," he said, bracing his hands over the counter outside my legs.

"I guess so," I replied, scooting off the edge of the counter, since the backs of my legs were falling asleep. Bad idea.

Because nothing was working the way it was supposed to, and I fell off. Jude's arms wound around me, keeping me steady.

"Looks like I showed her," I said, gripping Jude's arms as the sensation drained back into my legs.

His eyebrows squeezed together. "Showed her what?"

"That she better keep her hands and sights off my boyfriend," I replied. My mind was still foggy.

Jude's eyebrows pulled tighter for a moment before his whole face flattened. "That's what this whole thing is about," he said, running his eyes down my dress, which was still rolled up to my waist. "Isn't it? This whole night has been about Adriana. Not about me."

Uh-oh. I shouldn't have said anything.

"No, this was for you," I said, quickly pushing my dress back down.

"Don't lie to me, Luce," he said, the muscles in his jaw going taut. "Everything—the dress, the little smiles and flirty eyes, the thong, the freaking orgasm in the bathroom as Adriana pops in, 'coincidentally' followed by Holly—it was all just some jealous girlfriend play."

"No. The bathroom was one big, unplanned, pretty awesome surprise," I argued back. "At least up until right now. There's nothing awesome about my boyfriend calling me a lying, jealous girlfriend."

"So this wasn't planned," he said, waving his finger around the room, "but everything else was. And you sure as hell didn't mind when Adriana got an eyeful of us going at it."

Why was he being like this? Jude rarely raised his voice at me—everyone else, sure, but not me. And the fact that he was now doing so because of Adriana made me equal parts outraged and sad. "If that's what it takes—her seeing you doing me over every porcelain surface in the goddamn state—then yes! I definitely don't mind!" Great. Now I was shouting.

He pressed as far away from me as the bathroom allowed. The stark contrast between the intimacy we'd just shared and him wanting to separate himself as far as possible made my heart ache. "So still, after everything, after all this time"—he paused, inhaling through his nose like a bull ready to charge—"you still don't trust me?"

He waited for my response, but I didn't have one just yet. His question threw me, not at all what I was expecting. Was that it? Did I not trust him? My gut response was, *Of course I do,* but then why had I been acting like such a crazy, paranoid girlfriend? If I trusted Jude, would it matter if every Adriana in the world threw herself at him?

I didn't want to admit my answer to that question. Even to myself.

"Yeah," he said, moving toward the door and opening it, "that's what I thought." He looked back at me. "Here, you can have these back now." He tossed the underwear at me. "Well played. So glad I could be a pawn in your little game."

"Jude!" I called after him.

"Leave me alone, Lucy!" he shouted back, disappearing down the hall.

He only called me Lucy when he was hurt or pissed. I guessed he was a lot of both. But leaving him alone was *not* going to happen.

Not when I knew a welcoming set of arms was lurking around the corner, more than happy to take over.

SEVEN

The only time I wasted was the thirty seconds it took to put my underwear back where it belonged. Winding down the hall, I did a quick scan of the main floor. Gazing into the packed room, I didn't see him. If he wasn't in plain sight . . . my stomach went into overdrive as I wondered who was consoling him and where they were locked away.

Lunging up the stairs, I rushed down the hallway to Jude's room. It was irrational to think Adriana had already clawed her way into Jude—on some level I knew that—but there was no stopping my crazy runaway-train mind.

I didn't knock before barging into his room, though I wasn't sure I wanted to see what I'd find inside. I sighed in relief when I found it dark and empty. Just as I was about to leave and search the next place, I noticed a figure crouched on the floor beside the bed.

His elbows were propped onto bent legs, his head hanging between them. He looked broken. What had I done to him?

I closed the door behind me and crossed the room.

"Jude?"

"Go away, Luce," he said so softly it was almost a whisper.

"No," I said, coming around the side of the bed, closer to him.

"Go away," he repeated, clasping his fingers around the back of his neck.

He'd never said those words to me. Ever. And now I'd heard them twice in less than five minutes.

I kicked off my shoes and scooted next to him on the floor. "No," I said again. "You're pissed at me and I'm pissed at you. Let's deal with it."

"Yeah, I am pissed at you," he said, looking at the floor. "But I've got a good reason to be. Why in the hell are *you* pissed at *me*?"

I opened my mouth to reply.

"And your answer better not have 'Adriana' in it."

I did not like the way her name sounded on his lips. "Damn right my answer has her name in it."

Jude shook his head. "So you're pissed at *me* because of *Adriana*," he said, not hiding his sarcasm. "A girl I haven't even touched or looked at in any wrong way. Great. That makes a shit ton of sense, Luce."

I could feel my temper flaring. "Don't play dumb," I said. "Like you don't know she'd let you touch her any way you wanted."

Jude scoffed at me. "Yeah, well, just so *you* know, there's no shortage of girls here who would let me do whatever the hell I wanted to them. There's not exactly a lack of Adrianas in the world, Luce." He paused while I tried not to mentally calculate the number of women who'd jump on Jude any night of the week. "But you know what makes me say no every time? Why I don't even notice these other girls and their attention-grabbing plays?" He didn't wait for my response. "You, Luce," he said, his voice tired. "There may not be a shortage of Adrianas out there, but there's only one you. And you're the person I want to be with."

He was saying all the rights things, and honestly, he hadn't given me one reason to doubt him since the time I thought Holly's baby was his baby too, but I wasn't ready to give in. Not after the load of shit Adriana had strewn my way all day long.

"You let her do your laundry, Jude," I began, sort of wishing I had the brains to shut up when I needed to. "She cleans your room. You lead her into a damn room on your arm with hundreds of people watching." My voice was running away with me. "She runs her fingers over your clean, pressed underwear. Damn it, Jude!"

I was taking it all out on him. Everything I'd been bottling up today, when it would have been more constructive to find a dance floor and give it a run for its money.

His head twisted my way, and whether it was the darkness in the room or the actual color of his eyes, they looked black. "Did you not hear what I just said to you?" he said, his teeth clenched together. "Did you miss when I just professed that all I want is you? Even when you're acting like some crazy-ass girlfriend?" Narrowing his eyes at me, he hoisted himself up.

"Yeah, I heard that," I answered, leaping up beside him. "So I'm your girl. I'm the only girl you want to make moan in the bathroom. Yeah, I get it." My words were hurting him—I watched as each one etched a deeper wrinkle into his face. "But you let her take care of you like she's your old lady." Grabbing a handful of Jude's freshly made bed, I tore the covers off. "You might not want her intimately, but you let her into your life intimately."

Jude stared at me, like he didn't recognize the person standing before him. "Fine," he said, ripping the blankets curled in my hand away and tearing the rest of them off the bed. Rolling them into a ball, he tossed them across the room.

"Happy?" he asked rhetorically as he marched across the room to his dresser. Sliding the drawer open, he ripped it out and carried it over to the window. He opened the window and tipped its contents outside. His clean, folded boxers parachuted to the ground below. The drawer followed behind them.

"Happy now?" he asked again, raising his brows at me where I stood frozen beside his bed. Lunging across the room again, he ripped the second drawer from the dresser. Rushing back over to the window, he spilled his shirts to the ground.

"Happy yet?" He ran across the room, tore the last drawer out, and hurled the whole thing out. The sound of it shattering echoed back into the room.

Finally, he looked at me. His chest was rising and falling hard, his eyes were flashing—he was lost. "What else, Luce? What else do you want me to bust to shit?" he hollered, waiting for me. "Huh? Surely there's something else I can break to prove my love to you. What is it?" He was in a frenzy, as toeing the ledge as I'd seen him. All because of me. I loved knowing I had power over him, but not this kind of power.

"Jude," I whispered, barely able to make a sound. "Stop."

"Stop? Why?" he yelled, extending his arms and spinning around the room. "I'm proving my love for you. So come on, Luce. What else can I ruin so you'll be happy?"

"Nothing," I whispered, biting my lip.

"What was that?"

"Nothing," I repeated, looking at him. "This isn't what I meant, Jude. Why do you fly off the handle anytime I question you?"

The skin between his brows creased. "Why do *you*?"

That was a question I didn't have an answer to. I took him in, observing what my jealousy and insecurity had reduced him to. I was supposed to be the person who brought him comfort and supported him, but tonight, I'd done everything but. A tear escaped my eye.

Jude watched it fall down the side of my face. His face pulled tight. "Tell me what to do, Luce. Tell me what you want from me. Because I'll do it. I'd do *anything*," he said, putting his arms behind his neck and watching me like he was afraid I was going to disappear. "You want me to tell Adriana to go screw herself and never so much as look her way again? No problem. You want me to never talk to another woman for the rest of my life? I'll do it." Crossing the room, he stopped in front of me, grabbing the sides of my arms. "I'll do *anything*. Just tell me what to do." He held me close as he waited for my answer.

I didn't have one.

"You're all I've got, Luce. I'll do anything not to lose

you," he said, his scar pinching into his cheek. "Just tell me what I'm doing wrong and I'll fix it."

This man had been through enough. Why was I making him trudge through more shit?

"You're not doing anything wrong, Jude," I said, swallowing. And he wasn't. As boyfriends went, he was the dream. As companions went, he had the makings of a lifelong one. "It's me. I'm doing all the wrong tonight." I pressed my hands into the sides of his face, trying to rub away the lines wrinkling it. "I saw Adriana all wild for you, and I let my insecurities turn me into a crazy person. I trust you. I don't trust her."

He blew a breath through his mouth. "You trust me?"

My throat tightened that he had to ask. "Yeah, Jude. I trust you."

"You love me?"

"Always," I answered, stroking his cheeks.

"Then screw Adriana Vix," he said.

I arched a brow.

"Someone else who isn't mad for his girl can screw her," he clarified, smirking at me. "Don't let anyone come between us, Luce. This thing we've got going on is going to be challenging enough without the likes of an Adriana Vix complicating it."

"I know," I said, looking away. "It feels like sometimes

I'm just waiting for the bottom to fall out beneath us. You know?" I felt guilty for admitting it, but I was a realist, and couples like Jude and me had the odds against us.

"I know, baby," he said. "I know. When it does, though, we'll just grab onto a rope and wait it out."

I nodded, wondering if this was the kind of life Jude and I could expect from now on. Searing moments of passion, interrupted by misunderstandings, followed by soul-baring makeups. It wouldn't be a bad way to spend a life.

"Come on then," he said, running his hands down to mine. "Come to bed with me." Leading me over to the blanketless bed, he kicked off his shoes, scooped me into his arms, and crashed down on the mattress.

Rolling me onto my side, he pressed himself against my back, cocooning me between his arms and legs. "Arguing with you is exhausting," he said outside my ear, mid-yawn. "Let's never do it again."

"Okay," I lied. It was a nice idea, but one Jude and I would never realize if we lasted. People like Jude and me didn't make it through life without a screaming match every now and then; that was the reality. But reality was a lot easier to face with Jude wrapped around me the way he was now.

We lay like that for a while, silent and still, enjoying the warmth of each other. A breeze rushed through the window, caressing my face. I grinned.

"I hope you've got more underwear hidden somewhere," I said, poking my elbow into his ribs, replaying Jude tossing his drawers out the window.

"That would be a negative," he said in a sleepy voice. "I was out of clean underwear this morning."

"Wait," I said, suddenly feeling very awake. "Does that mean . . . ?"

"Yep," he answered, nuzzling deeper into my neck, already half-asleep. I'd give him a free pass tonight. He'd won a big game, made me feel things a girl shouldn't spread over the counter of a boy's bathroom, held his own in an argument with me, and managed to say the exact right thing to calm me down. He had a right to be exhausted.

Smiling, I tucked deeper into him. "That could have made things far more interesting in the bathroom."

I felt his smile curve against my neck before I followed him to sleep.

EIGHT

*H*is body wasn't wrapped around me—like he was sheltering me from the world—any longer, but he was close. Whatever bond we'd built in the tumultuous months we'd shared, last night we'd passed over into something new. Something bigger.

"I can feel you staring at me," I said, keeping my eyes closed and curling deeper into Jude's pillow. It smelled like him—maybe that's why my dreams were so sweet.

His hand curled over mine, lifting it to his mouth. "Sorry, Luce," he said, kissing my knuckles. "I didn't mean to wake you. Go back to sleep." Rotating my hand, he pressed another kiss into the fleshy underside.

"How's a girl supposed to sleep when you're doing that?" I smiled, opening my eyes.

His eyes were trained on me, metallic in the morning

light. One corner of his mouth curled up.

"She's not," he said, leaping onto the bed, strategically landing over me.

"Good," I said, wishing I could have one minute to brush my teeth and run a brush through my hair, but with Jude, these moments of carelessness came rarely, so I wasn't about to chance excusing myself while all his engines were firing. "Sleep's overrated."

His hand slid up my side, swerving in and out over my rib cage, before settling over the top of my chest. "Yes, it is," he whispered, kissing the area below my ear.

This was one hell of a wake-up call.

"Did you lock the door?" I teased, situating myself below him so the important parts were aligned. No one in their right mind would let themselves into Jude Ryder's bedroom when the door was closed. Not if they didn't want to wear a fist-size dent in their forehead.

Challenging my prior assumption, Jude's door exploded open the next second, bouncing off the wall.

"Ehh," Holly said, making a face and holding her hands over her eyes. "You guys are like a pair of damn rabbits."

Make that everyone but Holly knew better than to throw themselves into Jude's room uninvited.

"Didn't you two get enough of each other last night?" She was talking quietly, at least for Holly, and judging from the way she was screwing her fingers into her temples, she'd had a wild night.

"Nope," Jude answered, hoisting himself off me.

"Good morning, Holly," I grumbled, sitting up in bed. "Great to see ya."

"Don't you whine like a baby to me. You had him to yourself all last night, and now I need to borrow him for a few hours or else I'm going to miss my flight."

"Yeah," I said, crawling off the bed. "I've got a mess of homework to finish, too." Running my fingers through my hair, I plaited it into a quick braid, since it looked like there wouldn't be time for a shower. "It looks like you've got two girls who need your chauffeur services this morning."

"I live to serve," he said, an expression curving into his face that gave away what he was thinking. Or reliving.

I wasn't a blusher—the genetic code just hadn't built it into my system—but I thought I felt one creeping up my neck.

"All right, lover boy," Holly said, snapping her fingers. She winced, grabbing her temples again. "The airport. Sometime today."

I hurried around the bed, grabbing Holly's shoes she'd let me borrow, and pulled my bag down from the shelf in his closet. Grabbing his keys from the nightstand, Jude took my hand and led me to the door.

"It's about time," Holly whispered, digging through her purse.

Jude snagged Holly's suitcase and we worked our way down the hall, stepping over and around bodies decorating the floor.

"Looks like we missed out on some party," I said, peering at one comatose couple, wondering how in all acrobatics they'd worked their way into that position.

"I wouldn't say we missed out," Jude said, peeking back at me with a suggestive smile.

"I think this is the one I made out with like a sex addict on a bender last night," Holly said, leaning over one of Jude's teammates, who was still smiling in his sleep. "Or maybe it was that one," she said, toeing the hand of the guy across from the first and inspecting his face. "Yeah, definitely this one. His lips are the more swollen of the two. Speaking of"—rummaging through her bag, she produced a tube of ChapStick—"my lips are in serious pain."

"I thought you said you were in a hurry, Hol," Jude called up the stairs at her, keeping my hand in his. At the bottom of the stairs, a pyramid of bodies blocked the way. Leaping over it, Jude turned around, grabbed my waist, and lifted me over the human barricade. Waiting for Holly to make her wobbly way down, he lifted her over as well.

Jude's truck was parked a ways off, so we hoofed it.

Coming around the side of the house, we saw scattered clothing and splintered wood decorating the side yard. I stopped in my tracks, appraising Jude's yard-decorating skills.

"Someone had a visit from the anger monkeys last night," Holly said, stopping beside me.

Jude peered at me from the corner of his eye. "They most certainly did.

"Rage is a terrible thing," he added, crossing the lawn, but not before snagging a dark tee draped over a shrub.

I smirked at his back.

By the time Holly and I hauled our tired, slow-moving butts to Jude's truck, he already had Holly's suitcase in the bed and the door swung open for us. Peeling the white shirt he was still sporting over his head, he tossed that into the bed too. No wonder he never had any clean clothes. Lifting the black tee above his head, he paused, looking at me, his brows coming together.

"It's all right," I said, rolling my eyes. Just because I'd behaved like a jealous lunatic last night didn't mean I wanted to be reminded of it. They were his clothes, regardless of who'd washed and folded them.

"Just checkin'," he said with a faint grin before tugging it over his head.

Holly and I just stood there outside the truck, watching the show. Stuffing the shirt into his jeans, Jude stopped, looking up at us with confusion.

"What?" he asked, tucking in the back and giving me a devilish grin.

I averted my gaze, trying to look unimpressed as I climbed into the cab. "Oh, go 'what' yourself."

Holly chuckled. "You know, Jude, the older you get, the uglier you get," she said, winking at me as she crawled in beside me.

"Yeah, yeah," he said, climbing into the driver's seat and starting the truck up. "And the older you get, the meaner you get."

Grabbing my thigh, he slid me closer until we took up a space intended for one person. He didn't let go once the entire drive.

"Why does Thursday seem like it's never going to get here?" I groaned, stalling outside my dorm in Jude's truck.

"Because it will feel that way," he answered, brushing my hair over my shoulder.

I groaned louder. Holly had made it off on time and, while I'd willed the drive from the airport to New York to go slowly, of course it hadn't. The good-byes Jude and I were forced to make every Sunday never got easier. We went to schools nearly five hours apart, so the possibility of sneaking in an afternoon weekday visit was out of the question. When we said good-bye, it was good-bye for an eternal five days.

Except for this week. It would only be for three days, due to Thanksgiving break. It was truly a time to be grateful.

"So you're okay with celebrating with my dad and mom on Thursday?" I asked again, just to make sure. At the last gathering, Jude had been civil, as had they, but there was a strain between the two families that I doubted would ever slacken with time. Jude's father murdering my brother because my father had fired him was the kind of drama daytime television creators couldn't even conceive of. It was the kind of thing people didn't "get over" after a few family dinners.

"Luce," he said, stroking my face, "you're my family. Where you go, I go." He blinked, looking through the windshield. "There's no one else but you."

I didn't like to dwell on Jude's lack of family, because it made my heart hurt like it was now. Jude truly had no family. No parents, no siblings, no grandparents, aunts, or uncles. And not due to choice. Jude's family had all, one by one, abandoned him.

I knew, at the core of his anger and possessiveness of me, this was what he feared most from me: one day turning my back on him and walking as far away as I could get.

The ache in my heart deepened.

"Good," I said, trying to play it off like I wasn't hurting, "because we're a team, and teams don't let their members go to family holidays alone."

"Okay, team," he said, turning in his seat, stalling just as much as I was. Taking a glance at my dorm looming in front of us, he sighed. "Luce? What is it you really hate about Adriana?"

At the name, my claws came out. "What's not to hate?"

He shook his head in exasperation. "Come on. Just pretend I'm a clueless idiot."

I lifted a brow.

"I know, hard to imagine, right?" he said, grinning. "So spell it out for me. What. Do. You. Hate. About. Adriana?"

There were so many catty answers to this question on the tip of my tongue, but none of those were what Jude was looking for. He was searching for the truth. He wanted the truth, and, as much as I didn't want to give it to him, he deserved it.

He gave my hand a squeeze.

"The truth is, it's not *her* in particular I hate." I paused, biting my cheek. "What I hate is the idea that one morning you could wake up and realize that you've been wasting your time with me. And if that day is tomorrow, I know who's going to be the first one in line to take my spot," I said, taking a breath. "Adriana Vix."

Jude shifted closer and draped his arm over my shoulders. "God knows I love you, Luce, but you are delusional," he said, totally straight-faced. "Like world-record-setting, hardcore delusional."

I elbowed him. "It takes one to know one, Ryder."

"See? That's it," he said, waving his hand. "That's part of what makes us so great, Luce. I'm crazy. You're crazy. Together, we make our own brand of crazy."

I felt the skin between my eyebrows pinching. "Come again?" Other than hearing a whole lotta crazy, nothing else was computing.

"I could hold you prisoner here for the rest of the day and list everything I love about you, but that's only half of it," he explained, turning toward me. "The other half is something I can't put into words. Something I don't think I'll ever be able to. It's something that ties me to you, and you to me. Call it chemistry, call it fate, call it whatever you want. All I know is that I'm yours just as much as you're mine, Luce. That's the surest thing I've ever known."

I reminded myself to breathe. Who needed Shakespeare when I had Jude Ryder saying these kinds of things to me?

"So you can promise me you're not going to wake up tomorrow, or the next day, or next year and realize I'm not that big of a deal?"

His eyes came really close to rolling. "I can promise,

guarantee, swear, cross my heart and hope to die, make an oath—"

"I get the picture," I interrupted, grabbing his arm.

He stared hard at me. "Do you?"

"It's nice to be reminded every once in a while."

"Every once a day," he mumbled, prodding my sides.

"Lucky for me you put up with my delusional, crazy, insecure self," I said, laughing as he continued tickling my sides.

His eyes lightened as he moved closer. "Lucky for *me*."

Just then, my phone chimed. India. I groaned as I turned it off.

"Till Thursday?"

Back to reality.

I picked up where his sigh let off. "Till Thursday."

He leaned in, his eyes drifting down to my mouth. "Better make it a good one then."

I couldn't help but smile, despite feeling like shit. Wetting my lips, I leaned closer. I made it a good one.

NINE

The scent of patchouli and the beat of reggae swept through the hallway, alerting me that my roommate and friend, India, had gotten, was currently getting, or was about to get, her freak on in our dorm room. It was an every-other-day occurrence in my life.

If I was lucky, I could dodge in and dodge out with my books so I could study down in the commons area. If I wasn't, and the room started erupting with screams and grunts and snarls, I'd just have to wait it out. The last time I'd walked in on India with her man of the day, I'd seen things no God-fearing person should have to.

Stopping outside the door, I listened. Nothing but Bob Marley getting his groove on. "Indie?" I said, tapping on the door. "Is it safe to come in there?"

"Safe, little miss pure-and-prude," India shouted back.

Opening the door, the muskiness of patchouli almost floored me. India was draped over the chair we had stuffed in the corner, wearing her red silk kimono bathrobe, smoking something that probably wouldn't be kosher with the resident adviser.

"Have a nice time?"

"Eh-huh," she breathed, giving me a stupid little grin. "If you were five minutes earlier, we could have made this a three-way."

Throwing my bag down on my bed, I plopped into our rolling chair. "Sucks to be me."

India leaned forward, her dark skin still dotted with sweat. "Speaking of sucking," she began, pursing her lips together, "did you guys . . . ?" She made a few circles with her index finger.

"None of your business," I said, spinning a revolution.

"So you didn't," she said, leaning back

"Nope," I said, clucking my tongue, "we didn't."

"It does suck to be you," she said, chuckling.

"Oh, shut up," I said, grabbing the stuffed aardvark we kept propped on our computer desk and tossing it at her. "You're getting enough for all of us."

"Yes," she said, taking a drag, "yes, I am."

Giving the chair another spin, I stared up at the ceiling, stalling on the whole studying endeavor because, while India was the female equivalent of a man-whore, there was no else who could listen or offer better advice when it came to the complicated world of men than my roommate. Save for Holly, but she was stuck on a flight for the next couple of hours and I needed advice ASAP. Plus, India had helped Jude and me get back together in a way. Long story short, India had dated one of Jude's teammates over the summer, and when Jude found out the "infamous" India not only went to Marymount Manhattan, but had a roommate named Lucy . . . he was on the phone with India that day, scheming up a reunion. And the rest is history—kind of.

"How was Jude?" she asked, identifying my stalling tactics.

"He was . . ." I sighed, replaying the weekend. A lot of highs and lows. "He was Jude," I settled on.

"Roller coaster Jude," Indie said, making a *mm-mm-mmm* sound with her mouth. "Now, honey, that's one ride I'd never want to get off."

"I know," I said, starting to feel dizzy from the spinning. "I don't want to either."

"Then what's the problem?"

"The problem is the roller coaster," I said. "We're either on top of the world or knocking on hell's door. There's no in between. No breathing room. Just constant up and down at one hundred miles per hour."

It always felt good talking with India about my concerns with Jude's and my relationship. She never judged, just gave solid advice.

"I know, Lucy," she said, shifting in her seat, "but your man's a passionate person. Just like you are. If the two of you are together, you've got to accept the roller coaster as a way of life. You wouldn't want him to change who he is any more than he'd want you to change. The drastic ups and downs will be what spending your life with Jude will be like. That's a fact. You just have to ask yourself if it's worth it. Is what the two of you have together worth the sacrifice?" Her eyes narrowed on me, driving the message home.

I knew she was right, and I knew it was worth it, but I was human and couldn't help but want the unattainable. "I just wish I could trade in the roller coaster for a carousel. Able to anticipate what was around every corner, making the journey with less dramatic ups and downs."

"I get that," India said, nodding her head, "but that's not the hand you were dealt, baby. Jude was the hand you were dealt, and that man is no carousel, Lucy. That man is the super-duper-looper, Six Flags, knee-trembling roller coaster extraordinaire." She sucked in a breath.

"I know," I admitted, already feeling better.

Jude was a roller coaster—I was a roller coaster. Together we created that super-duper-looper thing. It was scary, standing on the ground and looking up at it, but if that's the ride I had to take to be with Jude, I'd be first in line.

"Hey, thank your stars your man ain't no kiddie bumper cars," India added, taking another puff before blowing out a smoke ring. "I dated a man once who was like that. The man who is solely responsible for why I don't date anymore. He even made love like the damn kiddie cars. Bump. Sputter, sputter." India sat up, jolting back and forth. "Bump. Sputter, sputter." I started laughing, watching her acting out the scene. "Bump. Sputter, sputter. Bump. Fizzle." Wrinkling her nose, she groaned, collapsing back into the chair.

Our laughter blended down the hall with Mr. Marley.

"Great practice today, Lucy," Thomas said, coming up behind me as I walked out of the auditorium.

"Well, it helps that my partner is one hell of a dancer," I said, nudging him as I wrapped my scarf around my neck.

It was the Wednesday before Thanksgiving, and the New York weather was already bringing it on. What had possessed a girl who believed sun was essential to life to go to school in a place where the winters ran frigid and long?

My pointes bounced against my body as I walked, reminding me why.

"Yeah, so, your boyfriend," Thomas started, looking uneasy just speaking about Jude, "does he know we're partners for the winter recital?"

Poor Thomas. He was a dancer, not a fighter. I would be scared out of my tights too if I was supposed to be lifting by the crotch the girlfriend of a boy who packed a mean punch.

"Not yet," I said, throwing my cap on too. I would be living in a state of hat hair from now until May.

Thomas cleared his throat, fidgeting with the strap of his backpack. "Are you planning on telling him?"

"Of course," I said, turning toward my dorm. I still had to finish one more assignment before the end of the day, and the sooner I tucked myself into bed, the sooner Jude would be here in the morning to spend four whole days together. India was flying back home to her parents' place outside of Miami, so we'd have the whole room to ourselves.

I wasn't planning on leaving it once. That's what takeout was for.

"When?"

I shrugged. I hadn't really given it much thought. "This weekend, I guess."

"Okay," Thomas said. "I just want to be prepared. It's

probably for the best he knows sooner rather than later. It will make the shock a little less . . . extreme."

"You've thought this out," I said, trying not to give away my amusement. "Good for you."

"Yeah," Thomas said, "if the dude almost beat my ass for helping you out of a corset, he will murder me on the spot when he sees our modern interpretation of *The Rape of Persephone*."

I moved telling Jude about our performance and the "encounters" Thomas and I would share onstage up to number one on the list. The more notice Jude had about it, the more time he could get used to the idea so he, as Thomas had put it, wouldn't murder him on the spot.

"Don't worry, you'll be all right," I said, stopping outside the dorm hall.

"I'd say I'll be anything but 'all right' after your boyfriend is done with me, but thanks for the vote of confidence." Heading down the sidewalk, Thomas waved. "Have a nice break, Lucy."

I would.

"You too," I called after him, rushing into the building, because I was twenty seconds away from breaking into a chatter fest.

India was already gone by the time I made it back, but

110

she'd left a gift behind. Lying on my bed was a black shopping bag, cascading with red and pink tissue paper. Not exactly Thanksgiving colors.

Tearing into the bag, I tossed the tissue paper behind me, peering inside. My mouth dropped as I pulled out the item on top. It was black, lacy, and had holes in places that were normally covered.

"India," I muttered, shaking my head. Tossing the lingerie off to the side, I grabbed the next thing in the bag. Something cold and hard. I pulled out a pair of hardcore handcuffs, complete with key, dangling from my finger. Throwing them back in the bag like they'd stung me, I rolled the top of the bag over and stuffed it into the depths of our closet.

I might be ready to take the next step with Jude, but I wasn't ready to go from A to Z in the same night. I'd be regifting these gems at Christmas to the girl who'd so carefully selected them for her resident prude.

I hurried through my last assignment and emailed it off to the professor by eight that night. After having a cup of hot tea and a microwave vegetarian burger for dinner, I turned off the lights and crawled into bed, hoping I'd fall into a deep sleep.

After tossing and turning for three hours, I gave up.

Sometime after midnight, I threw *The Outsiders* into the player and watched that and another classic bad-boy movie before I managed to nod off. My alarm was blaring less than two hours later and I couldn't push the snooze if I wanted to get some studio time in before Jude showed up.

So much for the recuperative qualities of sleep.

TEN

was on my third cup of coffee. Somewhere in between my second and third, I'd crossed the line from alert to jumpy. Edgy was better than comatose, right?

The knowledge that Jude would be arriving any time helped my outlook significantly. Once they'd booked their flight to NYC, determined to spend Thanksgiving with us, my parents had made lunch reservations at some fancy place downtown. I'd insisted that we didn't need anything fancy, but Mom had landed a big new account and things were looking up. No matter what I said, she hadn't relented, so the four of us were eating at some swanky restaurant.

Jude had already texted me, asking what I was wearing and wondering if this was a tie-required kind of joint. I'd replied, telling him it was a whatever-he-showed-up-in kind of a joint, because Jude always looked amazing. Tie or no tie.

I'd selected something fancier, a cranberry-colored vintage-style dress, because I'd been living in jeans and sweaters and it felt good to dress up. As I slid into my stilettos, a knock sounded at the door.

I danced across the room. Throwing the door open, I found Jude standing there, looking uncomfortable in his tie and dress shirt, holding his hands behind his back. His discomfort melted when he took a good look at me.

"You get more beautiful every time I see you," he said, drinking me in like he was trying to cement this moment in his memory.

"Thank you," I replied, curtsying. "And you clean up rather nicely yourself." I ran my fingers down his tie.

"It's Tony's," he said, guessing my thoughts.

"Tony has ties?" It didn't fit my picture of the charmer I knew.

"He's Catholic," Jude said, watching my fingers slide down the tie. "And his mom calls him every Sunday to make sure he went to mass. So yeah, Tony's got a shitload of ties."

"It looks nice on you," I said, letting the charcoal tie fall back into place.

"Tony had to help me tie it, because I didn't know what the hell I was doing," he said, popping his neck from side to side like the thing was strangling him.

"Do you have your bag?" I asked, not seeing one in view.

Jude's face fell. "What bag?"

My face fell right along with his. "The bag you were supposed to pack to spend four whole days with me," I said, wanting to pout. "That bag."

"Oh," Jude said, his arm reaching for something, "you mean this bag?"

Snatching it out of his hands, I tossed it onto the bed. There. Now we were set for the weekend.

"And this is also for you," he said, removing his other hand from his back. Another rose. A pink one this time. We were making progress; it still wasn't the red rose of love, passion, and in my book, sex, but it was a step in the right direction from the white rose of purity he'd given to me last time.

He chuckled as I continued to study the rose. "It's just a flower, Luce. Not the answer to all of life's questions."

Taking it from him, I rested it on my pillow. "Everything means something. Whether we want to admit it to ourselves or not."

Walking into my room, he stared at my bed before looking back up at me. He gave me a stupid little smile as he grabbed my coat hanging over the swivel chair.

"I suppose that's true," Jude admitted, holding my coat open for me, "if you're a woman. But for us men, a rose is a rose. And unless we're in love with a girl or hoping to get our brains screwed out of our ears, we don't go out of our way to get them."

Stuffing my arms into my knee-length wool coat, Jude slid my hair out from beneath the collar. His fingers just barely grazed my neck, but I felt his touch all the way down to my toes. Anticipation made it even more flammable.

"So which of those man reasons reduced you to buying a rose for a girl?" Cinching the coat's belt, I turned to face him.

He had that same smile on his face. He lifted his brows. "Both."

My stomach flopped and dropped.

Managing to compose myself, I reached into the depths of my closet and pulled out a box with a big silver bow on it. "I got you a present."

He stared at it curiously, like he wasn't sure what it was or what he was supposed to do with it. "It's not my birthday."

I rolled my eyes. "I know that." I held the large box out, waiting for him to tear into it like I'd thought he would.

"And it isn't Christmas. Yet," he continued.

"Jude," I said impatiently, "I know what day it is. And for your information, gifts can be given any day of the year."

"What's the occasion?" he asked, continuing to stare at the present. "Other than Thanksgiving."

"No occasion," I explained. "This is strictly a 'just because' present."

His head tilted to the side. "A 'just because' present?"

I got it then. His state of confusion. He wasn't used to gifts, least of all on-a-whim gifts. That realization made me want to shower him with a present every day for the next decade. Looked like my savings account would be a thing of the past.

"Just because I love you," I stated, setting the box in his arms.

He cradled it to him, as his expression lightened into what looked like excitement.

"Come on," I encouraged. "Tear into that baby."

Like it was both the first present he'd received and the last he ever would, Jude tore into that box in record time. Sliding the top off, he settled the tissue paper to the side. He stared at the contents for a few moments, again looking confused, before his stare turned into a gawk.

"Luce," he whispered, "this is a leather jacket." Pulling it out, he let the box fall to the floor. He ran his fingers over the distressed brown material. "An *expensive* leather jacket."

"It wasn't that much," I lied, waving my hand.

I'd gone out shopping yesterday, hoping to find something special for Jude. The standard slippers, or cologne, or wallet just weren't cutting it. Jude wasn't your slipper-cologne-wallet standard kind of guy. On the way back to my dorm, I'd been perusing a few windows of the designer department stores I never wandered into. Well, I'd never wandered into until I'd seen that leather jacket. It was like the designer had been envisioning Jude Ryder when he or she had created it. I didn't look at the price, just told the salesperson I'd take an extra large gift-wrapped.

I'd be forgoing my morning latte for the rest of the year, but as Jude slid into the jacket, I realized it would be totally worth it.

"Damn," I said in awe. "That jacket was made for you."

Jude shrugged his shoulders to adjust the coat into place. "This is one sweet-ass jacket, Luce," he said, zipping it up. Jude in that jacket was not doing good things for my libido or, depending on which way you wanted to look at it, was doing *phenomenal* things to my libido. "But the only thing made for me was you." The look in his eyes wreaked even more havoc on my libido.

"For a certified bad-boy jock, you've got one hell of a way with words."

He chuckled. "Thank you, Luce," he said, clearly moved. "For being who you are. For loving me. For the jacket. For *everything*."

"You're welcome," I replied, realizing I'd spent the best six hundred bucks of my life yesterday. Who cares if it meant

I'd be working both a day and a night job this summer to replace the money bleeding out of my savings account? "For being who I am. For loving you. For the jacket. For everything. Oh, and you're also welcome for what's about to happen later today." I arched an eyebrow, my eyes landing on my bed.

His eyes widened. Then, taking a deep breath, he gave his head a clearing shake. "Come on," he said at last, grabbing my hand and leading me out of the room. "We've got all weekend. Let's make it to Thanksgiving lunch, brunch, whatever it is, before the clothes start flying."

Closing the door behind us, I blew out a breath. "If we have to."

Jude chuckled as we made our way down the hall. "Since your parents kind of flew across the country so they could have dinner with their precious daughter and her son-of-a-bitch boyfriend at some yuppie restaurant, yeah, I'd say we have to."

"You make a lot of sense for a member of the male species," I said as we made our way down the stairwell.

Jude gave me a look that said, *Obviously*.

My heels clanged down the stairwell, filling the space with the echo.

"How in the hell do you girls walk in those things?" Jude said, studying the shoes with a wince.

"We have special powers that enable us to do so."

Jude stopped on the stair below me. "Yeah, well, special powers or not"—scooping me into his arms, he heaved me against his chest—"I don't want you breaking your neck on the stairs."

I wrapped my arms around his neck. "You're going to carry me down four more flights of stairs?"

"No," he replied, his eyes flashing down at me. "I'm going to kiss you down four more flights." As he lowered his neck, I lifted mine, and when our mouths connected, I wasn't sure how he was able to keep bouncing down the stairwell without collapsing, but I wouldn't have been able to. Maybe that's the real reason he'd decided to carry me.

After he'd stiff-armed the exit door open, a New York surprise was waiting for us. Airy flakes of snow swirled from the sky, landing on our faces. Jude looked up, taking his lips with him. The sky was cloudy, a grayish blue.

"Looks like a storm's heading our way," he said, carrying me to his truck. "Good thing I'm prepared." Kicking his new snow tires, he opened the door and dropped me inside.

I grimaced as I pictured my Mazda and its lack of severe-weather readiness. Snow tires were a foreign concept to me, and I was unequipped for the winter that was already here, it appeared.

"Don't worry, Luce," Jude said, guessing my thoughts as

he hopped in next to me. "I'll get you taken care of. I'll drive your car up to the shop sometime this weekend and get a pair of snow tires put on."

I didn't like that solution for a couple of reasons. "You're not going anywhere this weekend unless you count moving from the head of my bed to the foot of it," I began, peering over at him as he pulled out of the parking lot. He was smiling. "And I'm more than capable of taking care of my own snow tires. I don't need you to do everything for me."

His face twisted. "Why not?"

"Because," I answered.

"Because why?"

Because for a bunch of reasons, but I didn't feel like listing them off for the entire drive. So instead I scooted next to him and rested my head on his shoulder. "Just because."

The drive to Soho lasted all of twenty minutes, but my head tucked into Jude's neck with his arm hanging over me made the drive go by even faster.

"This the place?" Jude asked, inspecting the restaurant, which seemed to be built with windows, as we rolled by.

"This is it," I answered, looking for my parents. They'd flown in earlier this morning and said they'd be getting situated in their hotel before meeting us for lunch. Jude was visibly uncomfortable, continuing to stare at the place like he didn't belong.

121

"Hey," I said, resting my hand on his leg, "you all right with this?"

Of course I wanted him to share Thanksgiving with my family, but not if it meant he was uncomfortable the whole time.

Maneuvering his truck into a tight spot on the street, he glanced over at me. "Yeah, I'm fine." He grabbed my hand and kissed it before turning off the car. "You're my family. I go where you go, Luce."

That warm feeling that seemed ever-present when Jude was around melted through me. His words were as skilled as his hands. I knew then the plight of riding the roller coaster was worth being able to call the man beside me mine.

Coming around my side, Jude swung the door open for me, and instead of lending me a hand, he scooped me back up into his arms. Pressing a warm kiss into my forehead, he carried me across the snow-white street and didn't set me down until we were standing in the foyer of the restaurant.

We were both laughing, consumed by each other, so the patrons and restaurant staff staring at us like the circus had just come to town didn't register with either of us right away.

"Sorry," I said, clearing my throat.

After setting me down, Jude wrapped his arms around me. "I'm not," he said loudly, the words echoing through the high-ceilinged foyer.

And then he was dipping me low to the ground, his eyes smiling down on me before his lips made slow work of unfreezing mine. As soon as they melted into submission, he leaned back. Smiling down on me, he whispered, "I'm not," before lifting me back into a vertical alignment.

The room was spinning, and now the onlookers were exchanging small smiles. A few of the men even tipped their martini glasses at the two of us.

"Name under your reservation?" the petite, red-haired maître d' said flatly. Fine. I'd be giving her the stink eye if a man like Jude had just dipped her to the floor, not caring if the whole world saw how crazy he was for her. Being Jude's girlfriend was worthy of stink eyes near and far.

"Larson," I answered, giving her a sweet smile while I wrapped both hands around Jude's arm.

As she checked her book, her eyes darted back to where my hands were affixed to Jude. "Table twenty-two," she barked to the person beside her.

"Right this way," the hostess said, leading us into the dining room.

"Thank you," I said, still smiling as we walked past the redhead, who was watching every rolling step Jude's ass made. *Stare all you want, honey, because the man is mine.*

My parents stood up from the table as soon as they saw us crossing the expansive dining room. They looked relaxed, both getting closer to resembling the parents of my youth. The parents they'd been before my brother's tragedy had changed us all into people we didn't recognize.

Jude held my hand tight in his, kneading it like it was a worry rock. I understood why. Even for me, pre–financial family crisis, this place would have been a bit out of the Larson family league, reserved for birthdays and special occasions. But for Jude, someone who'd come from a poor family, then spent five of his teen years in a boys' home, where hot dogs and canned vegetables were an every-night occurrence, this restaurant was like being in a foreign country.

A foreign land where the citizens were staring at him, a leather jacket over his one-size-too-small dress shirt stuffed inside a dark pair of jeans with cuffs fraying over old Converses, like he was an unwelcome tourist.

I stiffened, gripping his hand tighter and glaring at a few of the worst offenders as we passed.

"My Lucy in the sky," Dad said, opening his arms as we approached.

"Hey, Dad," I replied, letting go of Jude's hand to give him a hug.

"Happy turkey day," he said, squeezing me tight.

"Gobble, gobble," I said, smiling over at Mom.

"Hi, sweetheart," she said, her face looking younger than the last time I'd seen her. Some of the deep wrinkles had ironed out, and instead of looking perpetually pissed off, she was placid all the way.

Moving from Dad to Mom, I gave her a hug.

"Hey, Jude," I heard Dad say, a smile of pure enjoyment in his face. "Sorry, that just never gets old."

"Hi, Mr. Larson," Jude said formally, shaking hands with him. "Happy Thanksgiving."

Looking over at my mom, Jude cleared his throat. "Thank you for inviting me," he said, shifting his weight, his face looking uneasy. Coming around the table to him, I grabbed his hand up again and he visibly relaxed. This was going to be harder for Jude to get through than I'd anticipated. I'd hold his hand all afternoon if that's what he needed.

My mom came around the table, and stopping in front of Jude, she rested her hands on his shoulders. "We were glad you could make it," she said, her voice soft and her smile just sad enough to guess at what was going through her mind. Wrapping her arms around him, she pulled Jude into a hug. He looked as awkward as she did.

Greetings out of the way, we took our seats. I scooted my chair closer to Jude's and found his hand under the tablecloth.

"This is a fancy place," Jude said, gazing up at the painted ceilings and chandeliers hanging above us.

Dad's gaze followed Jude's, and even though it was only a little after noon and he was sitting in a high-backed chair that wasn't anything like his old recliner, Dad seemed alert—present in the moment. It was a nice change. "It's a little over the top, but the food's supposed to be amazing," Dad responded.

Jude nodded, glancing down at the restaurant's Thanksgiving Day menu. "*Really* fancy," he added, his eyes widening as he checked out the prices. "You'll have to let me pay for Luce and myself, Mr. Larson."

Both of my parents looked offended.

Jude worked part-time at a garage close to the campus to bring in a little extra cash. I didn't know how he managed to work twenty hours a week on top of his classes and football schedule and still make time for us, but he did it all. He said he was only able to do it because he didn't sleep. I didn't think that was much of an exaggeration.

"We couldn't let you do that," my mom said. "We invited you two here, and we insist on treating you."

Jude opened his mouth, which was as good as a wasted effort when it came to arguing with my mom, when Dad waved his hand.

"We've got it, Jude," he said. "It's the least we could do."

Jude's face went flat—a little color even drained from it—before his hand clenched around mine. "The least you could do because you ruined my family?"

My head whipped to the side. I'd known Jude was

uneasy, but I never would have guessed he was this upset. I was wrong. I'd pushed this on him. Too much, too fast.

My dad's shoulders sagged as he leaned back into his chair. "I meant the least we could do since you've taken such good care of our daughter."

Neither Jude nor anyone else had a chance to reply because our waitress arrived, her eyes automatically targeting on Jude. "What can I get you all to drink this afternoon?" she asked. Well, she asked Jude.

No one replied; we were all still in a shocked silence from Jude's mini explosion. So I broke the ice. "I'll have a pomegranate tea." I suppose I could have tacked on "please" for good measure, but the broad wouldn't take her moon eyes off Jude.

"I'll have a water," Jude said, staring at his menu.

"Oh, get something fun," Mom said, trying to lighten the mood. "They've got a special hot cider for today or—"

Jude glanced up, his eyes landing on Mom. "I'll have water," he repeated, his jaw tightening.

Shooting Mom a *leave it alone* look, I glanced back at the waitress. She was still fixated on Jude. "You know what? I'll have a water too."

Jude looked over at me, the muscles of his neck straining, and I grinned at him. He looked as distressed and ready to go crazy as a caged gorilla. I never would have guessed that Thanksgiving lunch with my parents would turn into Danger Central.

I should have known better.

"Make that four waters," Dad said, dropping his menu.

"Do you all know what you're going to order?" the waitress asked.

"We'll have four of the five-course Thanksgiving Day meals," Dad said, gathering our menus.

"I'm good," Jude said, shaking his head. "Thanks, though."

"Jude," I started, before he leveled me with a look that cut off my sentence.

"I'm not hungry, Luce," he said. "I'm good."

We'd gone from bad to worse in ten seconds. Things were heading downhill for the rest of the afternoon if we continued at this rate.

"Son—," Dad started, nothing but concern in his voice, but Jude cut in.

"I'm not your son," Jude said, his jaw clenching. "The man whose son I am is in jail for killing your son. So don't pretend we have some sort of relationship that entitles you to refer to me as 'son.'" He rose up in his seat, shoved his chair back, and marched away from the table.

I popped up and followed after him. Even at a fast walk,

I couldn't catch him. He had thundered through the exit before I had left the dining room.

As soon as I shoved through the door, I ran down the steps and into the street. "Jude!" I hollered at him, but he didn't hear me. He was pacing beside the bed of his truck, his hands on his hips and his eyes somewhere else completely.

Then, clutching his head, he kicked the wheel of his truck before driving his fist into the rusted bed. His other fist followed, until both were moving so fast I couldn't tell which one was responsible for each metallic note exploding in the air.

"Jude!" I ran across the street toward him, almost slipping on the fresh snow. "Jude, stop!" I said, grabbing one of his arms. He was so intent on beating the shit out of his truck I had to wrap both arms around one of his before I got his attention.

"Jude," I said, taking in a breath, "what are you doing?"

His eyes turned from the dents he'd hammered into his truck to me. They didn't turn from black to light like they normally did when I interrupted one of his bouts of rage, and having him look at me with those dark, tortured eyes made a chill crawl up my spine.

"I need you to leave me alone right now, Luce," he said, biting out every word.

"Like hell I'm leaving you alone," I said, not letting go of his arm.

"Dammit, Lucy!" he shouted, driving his other fist into the truck bed. "I'm not safe to be around right now."

"You wouldn't hurt me," I said.

"I never would intentionally, but I hurt things, Luce. I hurt people," he said, looking away from me. "I sure as shit don't mean to, but it's in the damn DNA. The only way I can protect you from *me* is if I recognize the times it's not safe to be around me, tell you, and you actually listen." His tone had turned from angry to pleading—almost begging. He was begging me to turn around and leave him alone, when these moments were when we needed each other most.

"I need to sort out my shit right now. I need to do this alone," he said, fitting his hand over my cheek, but he was careful, like he was afraid the contact might break me. "Tell your parents I'm sorry."

I lifted my hand and folded it over his, trying to press it harder against my cheek. I felt a warm wetness. I held my hand out in front of my face, then grabbed his. "You're bleeding."

"Barely," he said, pulling his hand away.

"Barely bleeding is a paper cut," I said, staring at his other hand, also dripping blood. "You're bleeding into the snow. You need stitches."

Opening the driver's-side door, I grabbed the keys he'd left underneath the seat. I didn't know where the nearest ER was, but we were in New York. A hospital couldn't be far off. "Get in," I instructed. "I'm taking you to get those gashes stitched up."

"No, you're not," Jude said, grabbing my waist and hoisting me out of the truck. "You're going to go back inside and enjoy the day with your parents."

"You need to get those looked at," I said, waving my hands at his.

"Leave it alone, Luce," he warned, letting me go and hopping into his truck.

"Stop acting like an asshole and think!" I said, kicking his door as he closed it.

Rolling down the window, he sighed. He wouldn't look at me. "I'm working on it," he said. "Will your parents give you a ride back to your place?"

"If I said no, would you stay?"

He didn't pause. "No," he said, starting the truck up. "But I would make sure a cab was here to drive you home safely."

Infuriating.

"Then yeah, they'll drive me home."

"Good," he said, nodding once. "I'll call you later. After I get my head back on straight."

I laughed with frustration. "If I had to wait for you to get your head on straight, I'd be waiting forever."

His face lined as his eyes closed. "I think I'm starting to see that too, Luce."

Dammit. That's not what I'd wanted him to reply with, although I should have guessed that was what he would go with. "I'm sorry, Jude," I said. "That's not what I meant."

He nodded. "I know, Luce. I know that's not what you meant." His grip tightened over the steering wheel. "But that doesn't mean it isn't true."

His voice made me wince. "Jude . . ."

Then, without looking my way, he eased out of the parking space, pausing and waiting for me to move.

Relenting, I took a few steps back.

"Bye," he whispered, heading down the road. My eyes filled with tears, but I wouldn't let them fall, because letting them fall was like admitting there was something worth crying over. Something worth crying over wasn't a place I wanted to visit when it came to Jude and me. So I didn't cry. I forced the tears back. I focused on the bloodstained snow at my feet, pushing away the thoughts that snuck up on me, whispering it was a sign of what was yet to come.

I did go back into the restaurant, ignoring the looks of curiosity and sneers of disapproval; I even managed to make small talk with my parents and eat a bite of everything that was served. I went through the motions, put on the *It's all good* face, but it wasn't. Every second that ticked by drilled another hole in my heart. I wanted to be with him, to comfort whatever needed comforting, to be assured we were going to be all right. That we'd weather this storm.

After lunch, I showed my parents around New York. We saw the sights, exchanged some more small talk, grabbed a light dinner from a street vendor, and the ache in my heart went deeper.

"Honey, are you sure you don't want to stay with us?" Mom asked, on the cab ride back to my dorm. "We've got an early flight tomorrow, but you could sleep in, order room service, and take a cab back."

"Thanks, but I've got a load of homework to get cracking on, and I need to rehearse for the winter recital," I said.

"You've got homework over Thanksgiving break?" Dad piped up.

"Tell me about it," I said, sounding as numb as I felt. "They're slave drivers here."

Dad made a clucking sound with his tongue, shaking his head. "This it, Lucy in the sky?" he asked, peering out the cab window at the dark dorm.

"Home sweet home," I said, as the driver rolled up to the curb.

"Are you going to be all right, Lucy?" Mom asked, as we exited the cab.

"She's going to be great," Dad answered for me.

I nodded, because that's all the lie I was capable of right now.

"Thanks for coming all this way," I said, giving my dad a hug. "And sorry things went so wonky."

"Life is wonky, my Lucy in the sky," he said, patting my cheek. "It's to be expected."

For someone who had been declared mentally unstable over five years ago, my father was a very wise man.

Mom wrapped me into her arms. "Everything will turn out fine, sweetheart," she said into my ear. "Men just need time to sort these things out. They don't have the need to talk the issue to death like we do."

Her warmth, coming after she'd been locked in ice-queen mode for the past five years, caught me by surprise. "Thanks, Mom," I replied. "That sounds like good advice."

"I'm the expert," she said. "I've lived it for five years now," she mouthed, glancing back at Dad.

"Have a safe flight," I said, giving them each a quick peck on the cheek. "See you at Christmas."

"Love you, sweetheart," Mom said as they watched me head toward my dorm.

They obviously weren't going to take their eyes off me

until I was locked safely inside. To parents whose children didn't grow up in New York City, it was a place where murder happened around every corner and a criminal was lurking in every shadow. I was pretty sure my mom had been clutching a canister of Mace when she stepped out of the cab just now, ready to blast it into the faces of whatever figures drifted out of the dark.

Sliding in my key card, I pushed the door open. Before stepping inside, I waved at them. They waved back, smiling at me, Mom tucked under Dad's arm, looking like the parents they'd been when I was in grade school.

At least one thing in my life was looking up.

The dorm hall was quiet. Silent. Most everyone was back home with their families, while the few who remained were likely out celebrating late into the night with their friends.

Shoving open the stairwell door, I walked down the empty hall, contemplating my next move. I was fighting every instinct to jump into the Mazda and not stop driving until I'd found Jude. I knew I should fight to stay put and do as he'd requested. Sit tight, give him some space, and he'd call me when whatever fit of rage that had risen had blown over.

But how long until he called? Did he mean tonight? Tomorrow? Next week?

Thumping my head into my door as I unlocked it, I

toyed with the idea of flipping a coin. Thankfully, I came to the conclusion that was a disaster waiting to happen. I wasn't going to let fate make my decisions for me. That was my job. I'd rather be the one to blame for making the wrong decision than fate getting all the credit when I made a right one.

Switching the light on, I stood in the doorway, staring at the bed where Jude's suitcase and the pink rose he'd given me hours earlier rested. The rose was already starting to wilt.

Staring at that flower, the pink petals curling at the ends as the life bled out of it, helped me make my decision. Turning off the light, I locked the door back up and ran down the hall. I wasn't going to let what we had die due to neglect.

I was down the stairs and out the door only a few minutes after my parents had left. I rushed to the garage, careful to keep from slipping and sliding through the snow. The last thing I needed right now was a sprained ankle. That would put me out of dance commission for weeks.

My car had been my one splurge here at school. Well, a *huge* splurge. In order to just pay the monthly parking garage bill, I'd worked so many doubles at the café back home last summer I still had nightmares about breaking coffee cups and spilling syrup on customers.

My feet were frozen by the time I crawled into the Mazda, so I blasted the heaters first. At the garage exit, I punched the gas a little too hard given the winter driving conditions. The car fishtailed a pattern in the snow before I got it under control. And I hadn't even made it down the block.

Taking a slow breath, I pressed down carefully on the gas, and the car behaved.

By the time I'd left the city, I was feeling just comfortable enough with driving in the snow to be dangerous, but the roads were quiet and would only get quieter by the time I made it to Syracuse. It would be well past two a.m., maybe even later with the roads, before I pulled into Jude's gravel driveway.

I didn't know that was where he'd gone—he could be anywhere—but that would be my starting point. I'd look in every nook and explore every cranny until I found him. I didn't care that he'd told me to leave him alone, to give him time to sort out his shit. I also knew there was truth in what my mom had said about men's issues with talking things through.

I didn't need to talk—I just needed Jude to know I was here for him. I just needed to have him hold me while he figured out his shit. I needed him to know I wasn't going anywhere and he couldn't send me somewhere that wasn't where he was.

I just needed to have him look me in the eyes and know

that everything was going to be okay.

It was after three by the time I cut the ignition outside Jude's house. The snow had made the trip difficult and added another hour to the five-hour journey. I wasn't tired anymore, though, because parked across the front lawn was Jude's truck.

The usual cluster of cars dotted the street and driveway—not a party-night showing—but there was always some sort of get-together, holidays no exception.

Walking across the lawn, I made sure to go slow because the falling temperatures had made most of the state of New York a thin sheet of ice. I still had my stilettos on, and they weren't exactly ideal shoes to be tramping through an ice field in.

I made it up the walk and stairs, and resting my hand over the doorknob, I exhaled, realizing I'd been in such a hurry to get here, I hadn't really planned out what I was going to say.

I didn't need to say anything, I reminded myself. I just needed to wrap my arms around him and let him know I was here for him. However he needed me to be. Just as long as it wasn't being left behind on some street in Soho.

I didn't knock, because no one would have answered. You didn't knock here, you just walked through the door like you owned the place.

A few guys were milling around in the living room, eating pizza and playing video games, but no one noticed me when I came inside. Jude wasn't among them, so I jogged up the stairs, hoping my search would end in his bedroom. I didn't need an audience for whatever Jude's reaction would be to me showing up in the middle of the night.

His door was closed, no sounds coming from it other than the stream of the shower. Twisting the door open, I stepped inside. I was already heading toward the bathroom when I realized Jude wasn't the one in the shower, causing billows of steam to drift into the room.

He was draped over his bed, in a drunk coma.

Buck naked.

His fingers were still wound around an almost empty bottle of tequila. My mind couldn't keep up with everything that was coming at it. Jude. Naked. Bed. Drunk. Tequila. Shower.

Just as my heart took a nosedive, the shower shut off. I wanted to turn and run out of his room and this house and pretend I hadn't seen any of it. I wanted to wake up tomorrow with a mind erased of everything from twelve p.m. yesterday to three a.m. today.

I heard the shower curtain slide open, and just as I was backing up toward the door, someone sauntered out of the bathroom. As naked as Jude and still wet from the shower,

Adriana shifted her gaze my way, her face falling for one second. And then it lifted into a smile. "Oops," she said, turning toward me so I could see every naked inch of the body Jude had enjoyed. "We weren't exactly expecting you."

I kept moving backward, not able to get out of this room fast enough. In my hurry, my hip smacked into the side of Jude's dresser. A picture frame fell to the floor, shattering.

The noise jolted Jude awake. Shaking his head, the first thing he noticed was the bottle he was clutching. His eyebrows came together. Examining his naked arms next, his eyes traveled down the length of him. Now, a frown. Then he saw Adriana, in all her naked, wet splendor, taking a break from smirking at me to shoot a wink his way.

He paled, and then, when his eyes swept my way, his face broke. Like mine had.

I wasn't going to lose it in front of her. I wasn't going to let her see that she'd won. Finally reaching the door, I threw myself out of it, already sprinting down the hall when Jude's shout rang after me.

"Luce!"

I didn't stop—I didn't even slow down. I would never stop or slow or sigh over him saying "Luce" again. Barreling down the stairs, I ran into a hard chest.

"Whoa," Tony said, grabbing hold of me. "Lucy? What

are you doing here?" he asked, looking down at me. "Why are you upset?"

Throwing a look over my shoulder, I dodged out of Tony's hold. I didn't see Jude, but his voice was getting closer.

"Luce!" Jude shouted again down the hall. "Wait!"

I didn't. I couldn't.

Rushing out the door, I leaped down the stairs, sliding almost the entire way to the Mazda. My hands were shaking, but I managed to pull the keys out of my coat pocket and start the ignition. As I punched the car into drive, a shadow eclipsed the yellow light streaming out of the open front door.

Jude.

I hit the gas, forgetting I was on a plane of ice. My tires spun, getting me nowhere.

"No, Luce!" he shouted so loudly I could hear it across the lawn and through the windows of my car.

Taking a breath, I eased down on the accelerator this time and gained some traction. Encouraging the Mazda forward, I picked up some speed.

Before I'd gotten more than a few car lengths away, I caught sight of Jude leaping down the stairs and running across the lawn after me. He was still naked, nothing but a pair of boxers clutched in front of his nether region.

Gripping the steering wheel, I pressed the accelerator lower, praying I wouldn't wind up in a ditch at the end of the road.

"Lucy!" he shouted, banging into the side of the car.

I screamed in surprise, hitting the gas harder.

Pounding on my window, he ran alongside the car. "Stop, Lucy!" he yelled. "Don't do this."

I couldn't look at him. I couldn't look at what I'd lost so soon after losing it. Keeping my eyes on the road, I bit my lip to keep from crying and shook my head before punching the accelerator.

He stopped being able to keep pace by the time I got to the end of the block, and even though I swore I wouldn't, I looked in the rearview mirror.

He was crouching in the middle of the road, his breath steaming up the night air, and his head hung like he was both praying and accepting his punishment.

ELEVEN

I don't know how I made it to the parking lot of a hotel outside Monticello in one safe piece, but I guess it had something to do with angels. There'd been numerous alerts coming through the radio advising people to stay off the roads, and if one had to go out for an emergency, to make sure they strapped on chains.

So the fact that someone who had never driven in snowy conditions managed to drive hundreds of miles without bending her snow-tire-less car around a median must mean the divine hand of providence was at work.

Grabbing my purse, I popped out of the car. My heels slipped and slid across the parking lot, but I was able to make it inside the lobby safely. The air was perfumed with coffee and some sort of chemical cleaner. But it was clean and it was somewhere Jude wouldn't be able to find me.

I knew he'd come looking—I'd been checking in my rearview mirror every mile, expecting to see the square headlights of his truck shining down on me, but they never had. But then again, who knows? Maybe I'd overestimated him. Maybe he got the whole chasing-after-me thing out of his system when he ran balls to the walls down the middle of an icy road, wearing nothing but a boxer loincloth. The thought made me more depressed. I wanted to be chased, in some part of me I didn't want to acknowledge—I wanted to know I meant more to him than giving up after a few minutes.

But then I remembered Adriana's glistening naked body and that triumphant smirk of hers, and I swore I never wanted to see Jude Ryder ever again.

I walked carefully across the lobby, like I was still walking on ice, and the receptionist looked up. Her smile was warm. "Good morning," she greeted.

"Hi," I replied because there was nothing "good" about this morning. "I need a room if you have one."

I hadn't realized this hotel might be full. The thought of getting back in the car and white-knuckling a few more miles to the next one made my stomach turn.

"We sure do," she said, thrumming her fingers over the keyboard. "How long will you be staying with us?"

As long as possible. To the end of time.

"Until Sunday," I said. I didn't want to be in my room or in a place I could be found until I absolutely had to be.

"Check-in isn't until three, so I'm technically supposed to charge you for four nights," she said, swiping a card key through a device.

"That's fine," I said, pulling out my wallet.

"But it's Thanksgiving weekend, and I like to give 'technically' a break on the holidays," she said, looking up at me with that smile again.

"Thanks," I said, handing her my card.

I didn't know how much it would cost. I didn't even know if the only room they had left was the presidential suite. I just had to crawl into a bed and let sleep take me over.

She took my card, studying my face. Her smile lined into concern. "Honey, are you all right?"

Great. I was a walking basket case. I suppose my red-rimmed eyes and puffy face gave it away.

I nodded. "Just tired," I said, wishing she could run my card faster so I could get on my way.

She handed me my card back. "You give us a call at the front desk if you need anything," she said, resting her hand over one of mine. Patting it, she gave me another smile. "Lord knows I love 'em, but men are one giant pain in the ass."

I didn't ask why in the entire population of hotel receptionists I'd wound up in front of the most perceptive one, because the irony of it just sort of fit the tone of the last twenty-four hours.

Trying to smile back, I tapped my card key on the counter. "Ain't that the truth," I replied, before heading toward the elevator.

I made it to the third floor; I even made it down the hall and into my room before the next batch of tears. For someone who loathed crying, I was eating a lot of crow today. Taking a few seconds to kick off my shoes and coat, I slid under the covers and closed my eyes. I was asleep before the next tear could fall onto my pillow.

I spent the next three days in my room. I slept almost all of Friday, watched the television unseeingly after that, and didn't order my first meal until Saturday afternoon, because I'd lost my appetite. Even at that, I had to force myself to finish half of my veggie on wheat sandwich. In between channel surfing and sleeping, I took showers. I preferred them to baths because I could pretend I wasn't crying when I was in the shower. I tried to find a ballet studio to get some of the pain sweltering inside of me out. Of course, not a single studio was open over the holiday weekend.

I'd turned off my phone when I woke up on Friday

because Jude had been calling it every half hour since earlier that morning. My guess was that he'd made it back to my dorm by then, only to discover I wasn't there, and was going nuts trying to figure out where I was or worried what had become of me on those roads.

Turning my phone off, I reminded myself that a man who slept with another woman didn't have the right to worry about me or be assured I was safe anymore.

I slept late into Sunday, wanting to delay the inevitable. The hotel had been like this warm security blanket, but it couldn't hide me forever. I had to get back to reality, and I sure as hell wasn't going to ruin my life over one guy who I shouldn't have let into it in the first place.

The ice and snow had melted by Friday afternoon, so the roads and my Mazda got along much better this trip. Now all I had to contend with was holiday traffic.

It was late when I made it back to New York. I told myself it wasn't because I'd been stalling, but because I'd wanted to take in the sights of the skyline from behind the windshield of my car. Of course I'd been living in a state of denial all weekend, so why should I stop now?

The garage was almost full again. Pulling into my assigned space, I turned off the car and gave myself a few long breaths before getting out. I couldn't put this off any longer.

Jude and his truck weren't anywhere in view, so maybe I'd been right and I hadn't been worth more than a few minutes' chase and a gazillion phone calls. The thought was one of the most depressing ones I'd had to date.

I still had on the same outfit I'd left the dorm in on Thursday, but it was crumpled, dirty, and in need of a trash can now.

I could smell the signs and faintly hear the sounds, even from the stairwell, that India was back. That was just what I needed. To curl up next to her while she made me some kind of hippie tea that contained I didn't want to know what, while I spilled my guts and she gave me some sage advice that was along the lines of siccing a voodoo witch on Jude.

Shoving open the stairwell door, which felt twice as heavy as it used to, I stiffened as soon as I turned down the hall. The same figure, in almost the same position I'd peered at in my rearview mirror three nights ago, was crouched down the hall, staring at my door like he was begging it to let him in.

I'd just taken my first step back toward the stairwell when Jude's shoulders stiffened, right before his head snapped my way.

"Luce," he breathed, saying it like it was a prayer.

I shook my head, my eyes filling with more damn tears as I kept backing away. I couldn't do this anymore. I couldn't do Jude Ryder anymore, because it was going to wind up being the death of me. Or institutionalization.

"Luce. Please," he begged, working his way into a stand. He wobbled, like he had run out of strength or was shit-faced drunk.

I kept backing away. It was the only way I knew to protect myself from him. I'd just keep retreating to the end of the earth if I had to.

"Luce," he repeated, his entire face twisting. Balancing against the wall, Jude took a couple of steps in my direction before his legs gave out, his whole frame collapsing onto his knees.

How I responded was instinctual, not rational. Rushing toward him, I had this flash of panic that he was dying. I'd never seen Jude weak; I didn't think it was in him. Vulnerable, sure, but never weak. And here he was, not able to support his own weight more than a step at a time.

Sliding to the ground next to him, I could tell right away that his lack of balance and coordination weren't alcohol-induced. His strained breath smelled only of Jude, and his eyes were clear.

Except when they lifted to meet mine, they clouded with some emotion that ran so deep I was sure I could never pinpoint it.

"God, Luce," he breathed, his breath coming in haggard

spurts, "don't do that to me again."

His arms folded around me, pulling me against him with all the strength he had left. It wasn't his normal embrace, the one that felt like those arms could shield me from the whole world; this one was hollow and even a bit awkward.

I pushed away from him, assured he wasn't going to die anytime soon, and my sorrow morphed into anger. Partly to do with him being here when he didn't have a right to be here anymore, and partly because I had to look on what I'd lost again. His face lined with pain when I pushed him away.

"Don't ever do that to *you* again?" I spit the words back at him. I didn't care how weak he was; he didn't deserve even an iota of mercy. "Don't ever do that to *you* again?" I couldn't seem to get anything else out.

"Yeah," he said, staring at the ground, "don't do that to me again. Do you know how goddamned worried I've been about you?" His chest was heaving with his words, like oxygen wouldn't take up residence in his lungs. "Do you know how many times I've searched this city over, making sure you weren't dead in some back alley? Do you know how many hospitals, police stations, and news stations I called every hour to make sure they hadn't found you at the bottom of some ditch?" His eyes lifted back to mine, and they flashed onyx. "So, yeah, don't you ever do that to me again."

"Fine," I said, giving his chest another shove. For the

first time, I could actually move him. "I'll stop doing *that* to you when you stop screwing skanks behind my back. Oh wait, I'm done with you and your cheating-ass ways, so you can screw whoever the hell you want." Shoving him again, I bolted up, lunging toward my door. I needed a buffer between us right now, preferably a state or two, but I'd have to settle for a dorm room door.

"You are not done with me," he said, gritting his teeth as he tried to stand.

"Oh yes, I am. I'm so done with you, Jude Ryder!" I shouted, spinning on him once I'd thrown open the door. "I'M DONE IN!" I slammed the door shut, but it bounced right back. Jude had wedged himself inside the doorway, and I'd managed to slam that door hard into the side of his face.

He grimaced, but it looked like it was more due to the kind of pain that wasn't physical.

"Hell and Hades, you two!" India shouted, springing up from her chair. "Stop making a scene. You're not the first couple to have a lover's quarrel, so stop acting like it."

Pushing me to the side, she leaned over Jude, glancing down the hall. "Sorry," she called out, "we're working out some issues down here. We won't keep y'all up all night."

Waving down the hall, she glanced down at Jude, who was leaning into the doorway, breathing like he still couldn't

151

catch his breath and staring at the floor like he was waiting for it to swallow him up. Grabbing Jude by the shoulders, she pulled him inside the room. "Get in here, you crazy son of a bitch."

Once Jude was inside, she shut the door and slammed her back against it. Exhaling, she looked over at me where I stood at the foot of my bed, arms crossed and looking everywhere but at Jude.

"Hear the man out," she ordered. "He's earned it, and you deserve it."

"Wait"—my eyes flashed to India's—"you've already talked with him? You actually believe the pile of lies he gave you?"

India wasn't gullible and believed that, as a species, humans weren't to be trusted, so whatever Jude had said to her had to have been impressive.

One big, fat, impressive lie.

"That's right. When I got back and found him camped out in the hall, refusing to leave, I sat down and heard him out," she said, looking at me like I was behaving like a brat. "You got a problem with that?"

"Only a few million," I smarted back. "*Friend*," I tacked on to drive in the guilt.

It didn't work.

"Listen, friend," she said, arching a brow. "He's here. You're here. Talk this shit out, and then you can go back to hating his sorry ass when it's all out there on the table."

She walked toward me and wrapped her arms around me, giving me one long, tight squeeze. Her long, gold earrings chimed against my shoulder. "Talk. Listen. I know it seems hard, but it really isn't," she said, moving toward the door. "I'll be in the commons if you need me."

Leaning over Jude, she patted his cheek. He didn't respond. "Here's your chance. Don't waste it."

Opening the door, India glanced back down at Jude's crumpled form, frowning. "See if you can get this man to eat or drink something, Lucy. He's going to be knocking on death's door if he doesn't get some fluids in him. And you better drink, you crazy bastard," she said, toeing at Jude's leg. "Because a person can only go seven days without fluids before their system shuts down. I'm guessing you're on day four."

Before closing the door behind her, India gave me a small smile of encouragement, and then it was just Jude and me.

As pissed as I was at him, a nagging worry tormented me. He was weak, weary, barely able to catch his breath, staring at the floor without seeing it.

"You really haven't eaten or drunk anything in four

days?" I asked, moving over to the mini fridge.

"I can't remember," he answered, his voice as weak as the rest of him.

"Damn fool," I muttered, collecting a couple of bottles of water and a bar of chocolate India and I kept stashed in the back for emergency purposes. A man about to pass out from not eating in days qualified as emergency purposes.

Falling to my knees in front of him, I unscrewed the lid from one of the bottles. "Here," I said, lifting it to his lips, "drink."

It wasn't a request.

He didn't move; his head just hung there, his fists clenching and unclenching over his thighs.

"Jude," I said, lifting his chin until we were at eye level. "Drink this. Please."

His eyes were almost as hollow as his embrace had felt in the hall. Something twisted in my gut, something that ran deeper than anything else had.

He parted his lips, and I lifted the bottle to his mouth and tilted it so a steady stream would fall in.

He swallowed, keeping his eyes locked on mine, gulping down everything I was giving him until the bottle was empty.

I had to look away, because I couldn't look into those eyes any longer. The gray had drained out of them, leaving nothing but black behind.

"Better?" I asked, tossing the bottle to the side and handing him the next.

He nodded, looking like he was about to pull me to him.

"Good," I said, lifting my hand and slapping him across the cheek. I hadn't realized I was going to do it, but it felt damn good.

At least it felt good until he flinched, his eyes closing as a red hand mark blossomed over his cheek.

"I'm sorry," I said, leaning toward him and inspecting his face.

I'd just hit Jude. Hard. And I hadn't even known I was about to do it.

Hang on, because this roller coaster had reached the summit and was about to race straight down.

"Jude, God," I said, fussing over his face. I was all emotion and instinct—reduced to a monster. "I'm sorry."

"Do it again," he whispered, his eyes still closed.

"What?" I said, hoping I'd heard him wrong or was mistaking what he meant. "No."

"Do it"—he opened his eyes and locked them onto mine—"again."

This roller coaster was going down. All the way down. "No," I said again, wondering if my slap had knocked something loose.

"Dammit, Luce," he hollered, grabbing my wrist as I tried to scoot away, "hit me again!"

"No!" I was shouting now too. "Let me go, Jude!"

"Hit me!" he yelled, raising my hand above him and pounding it down against his face. "Again!" Grabbing my other hand, he flattened it and drove it into his other cheek.

"Stop!" I cried, trying to pull my wrists free of his grasp. His hands formed liked vises over mine, not letting me go. He drove the other palm into his face, and then the other. "Stop," I whimpered, my throat contracting around my sobs.

He didn't. Hit after hit, Jude slapped my hands against his face until they were tingling.

"Jude, stop," I cried, my sobs rocking me. His cheeks were red, capillaries broken on the surface. "Please."

Then, as suddenly as he'd started, he freed my hands, letting them fall back into my lap. They stung, like hundreds of needles were poking at the surface, but what I felt inside hurt the worst.

I loved the broken man kneeling in front of me—loved him like I never would love another. But I couldn't be with him. For plenty of reasons, this latest episode only one of them.

"Feel better?" he said, falling back, using my bed as a backrest.

"No," I said, wiping my face with the back of my coat, looking down into my open hands like I couldn't believe what they were capable of.

"Me neither," he said, rubbing his hands over his face.

His breathing had grown shallower, and the parts of his face that weren't red were white and clammy. I'd never seen Jude so frail—never imagined him this way.

"Here," I said, tossing the chocolate bar at him. "Eat that."

"I thought you didn't care," he said, turning the bar over in his hand, inspecting it.

"I don't," I lied, settling into a more comfortable position on the floor. "Just eat it. I don't want you passing out, because it would take a half-dozen guys to move you."

One corner of his mouth lifted as he unwrapped the bar. Breaking a chunk off, he tossed it at me. "You look like you need sustenance as much as I do," he said, breaking off another piece. "I'll eat if you eat."

I sighed, knowing he was right, as much as I didn't want him to be.

"Fine." Taking a bite, I let the chocolate melt in my mouth.

Lifting his piece at me, he stuffed the whole thing in his mouth. He chewed it, staring at me as if he was contemplating his next move. "I didn't screw Adriana, Luce."

I almost choked on the bit of chocolate still melting in my mouth. He wasn't going to ease our way into this conversation. He was charging the red flag like a bull.

"Sure you didn't," I said, sliding my shoes off and tossing them across the room. "She just needed to borrow your shower. While you snoozed naked on the bed. With an empty bottle of tequila in hand."

The muscles of his neck tightened, his jaw following. "I didn't screw her, Luce," he repeated.

I laughed, one clipped note. "You were drunk, Jude. Shit-faced drunk," I said, trying not to visualize the whole scene in my mind again. "How the hell would you know?"

I was insulted that he'd led with the whole denial act. Jude knew I wasn't a gullible girl, and the fact that he was treating me like one now was just downright insulting.

"How the hell would I know?" he repeated, his face screwed into disbelief. "How the hell would I know, Luce?" Okay, now he was looking insulted. "I know because even if I drank every last drop of alcohol in every seedy bar in this town, there's only one girl I'd want to crawl into bed with. There'd only be one girl I could even fantasize about going to bed with."

"Let me guess," I mused, tapping my temple. "Adriana Vix?"

Jude pounded the floor with his fist. "Would you stop being so damn difficult?"

"Would you stop screwing manipulative bitches behind my back?" Low blow, but that's where I felt like hitting right now.

"I can't stop what I never started," he said, popping his neck, attempting to defuse the ticking time bomb from going off again.

"So you're telling me a naked, freshly showered Adriana Vix just magically appeared in your bedroom?" I hoped it sounded as preposterous as it was.

"Would you believe me if I told you what happened?" he asked, keeping his words slow, his muscles relaxed.

"No," I snapped, "but I'm sure it will be highly entertaining and quite imaginative, so please, tell away."

He took in another breath, really trying not to react to me baiting him.

"After I left the restaurant, I drove back to my house. I was pissed and angry at myself for ruining the day, so I grabbed myself a bottle of tequila and went upstairs and sulked in my bedroom until I was drunk."

"Shit-faced drunk," I clarified.

"Luce"—he dropped his gaze to me—"you and I both know it would take a hell of a lot more than a bottle to get me shit-faced."

So what if the man could hold his liquor? Not on that day. Not on an empty stomach. Not after he'd left his girlfriend in the middle of a snowy street.

"I was buzzing for sure, but when I crawled into bed that night, I was alone. And I at least had a pair of boxers on."

"So Adriana slipped into your room, stripped you, positioned you, and hopped into the shower?"

"Maybe."

"And I have 'dumb' tattooed to my face where?" I asked, glaring over at him.

"I've never once treated you like you were some dumb broad, Luce, so don't go there now," he said, shouting. "I'm telling you what I know happened, I'm admitting what I don't know, but I swear to you, on your brother's grave, that I did not take Adriana Vix to bed with me that night."

I recoiled from the words, scooting farther from him. "Don't you bring my brother into this," I warned, lifting my finger at him. "Don't you swear on his grave, you lying bastard!"

"All right," Jude said, exhaling through his nose. "I won't swear on anyone's grave. I'll just give you my word. I didn't do it, Luce. I love you. I'll only ever love you." The pain flashed through his eyes again. "I need you to believe me."

I laughed. "Too damn bad."

Dropping the half-eaten chocolate bar to the side, he exhaled. He was tired and drained, maybe even more than I was.

"Then I need you to trust me, Luce." Looking up, he met my eyes, and I didn't need words to read his meaning.

Trust. What I hadn't given him months ago. What I'd paid for by not giving it to him. What I'd promised him he'd always have.

And this was Jude's low blow. Asking me to trust him, knowing I couldn't deny him this when I had before. I knew what I'd seen, so I couldn't believe him. But I knew *him*, and because of that—no matter how preposterous this whole denial thing was—I made up my mind to trust him.

"Fine," I breathed, realizing trust was as painful as love.

Finally he could stop holding his breath. His whole body relaxed. "So we're good?" he asked so softly it was like he was afraid of the answer. "We're going to be able to make it past this?"

My hands were shaking, because this was it. The end.

"I trust you, Jude," I began, focusing on my trembling hands because I couldn't watch his face crumble again, "but I can't do this right now. I need a break."

I had to pause to collect myself before I could go on. "I

can't keep doing this up-and-down, never-knowing-what's-going-to-be-around-the-corner thing. I need some time to get myself right. To figure out what I want and how and if we fit into that picture. I need . . . time."

He'd stayed silent, unmoving, the entire time, letting me get out what I needed to.

"Luce," he said after a minute of silence, "are you saying what I think you're saying?"

His voice almost made me break down into sobs again. "Yeah," I said, turning my hands over. "I think so."

He sucked in a breath, his head falling back against my mattress.

"I just need some time right now, Jude," I rushed, wanting to give him a scrap of hope I knew wasn't there to give. "I need a break from the tornado you and I create everywhere we go."

"How much time?" His voice was a whisper, his own gaze focused on where my hands shook in my lap.

"I don't know," I answered. "A month. Maybe more."

"A *month*?" he gasped, punching the floor again.

"I don't know, Jude. I just don't damn well know right now," I said, on the verge of losing it again. "I'm sorry."

And I was. Despite whatever had or hadn't happened in Jude's bedroom Thursday night, I didn't want to hurt him. I didn't want to be the one responsible for the pain in his voice or the agony on his face.

He studied me, silently watched me. For what felt like forever. His eyes didn't miss a thing.

Crawling across the floor to me, his hands folded over mine in my lap, where they still shook.

"Okay," he said, his voice tight. "Take your time. Take as much time as you need. I'll be here when you're ready. No matter how long it takes. I'll always be here, Luce. I'm yours," he breathed, squeezing my hands, "forever."

He stood up, looking down at where I sat, just keeping it together by a thread, and stared at me. Like the idea of turning and walking out that door was crippling. Leaning down, he kissed the top of my head.

"Love ya, Luce," he said. "And I'm sorry my being in your life has made it so difficult. And I'm sorry I'm a piece of shit trying to feel his way out of being such a piece of shit." Opening the door, he paused before closing it behind him. "I'd do anything to make you happy."

As soon as the door closed behind him, my eyes flitted toward it, wishing I could take back everything. But I knew I couldn't. I couldn't keep doing this to myself. It wasn't healthy feeling these kinds of searing emotions on a regular basis.

I sat there in the same position, telling myself I'd made a huge mistake, only to remind myself two seconds later I'd done the right thing. I wasn't sure how long I'd been play-ing devil's advocate with myself when a tapping sounded outside the door.

"Come in." My throat ached and my voice was hoarse.

India stuck her head in, frowning when she saw me on the floor. "Did that bastard just break your heart?" she asked, stepping inside and kneeling beside me.

I shook my head. "No," I said, "but I think I might have just broken his."

"You two," she said, hanging her head. "When are you going to get your shit together, huh?"

My hands had stopped shaking, but they were numb. Dead.

"Maybe never," I answered. "Maybe we were never meant to be together in the first place." Saying those words hurt my throat worse than the sobs had.

"Lucy, Lord knows I love you and you're my vanilla-bean sister, but you can be an idiot sometimes."

My head whipped up. What I needed from India was compassion and a shoulder to cry my eyes out on. Not another voice telling me I'd just made the biggest mistake of my life.

"When are you going to stop looking at all the reasons you shouldn't be together and start focusing on the reasons you should be?" she asked, her eyebrow ring bouncing with her eyebrows.

"India," I said, "for all intents and purposes, he screwed my arch-nemesis. Any reasons we had to be together kind of flew south with his boxers."

"Is that what Jude admitted to?" she asked, plopping down beside me. "Making your arch-nemesis pant?"

"Of course he didn't admit to that," I snapped, glaring at the half-eaten chocolate bar on the floor. "He said he didn't do it."

"Then shame on you," India said, her eyes narrowing at the same time her arm roped over my shoulder. "If you say you're going to trust your man, then trust your man. Don't revoke that privilege when he needs it most."

"Oh, come on, Indie," I said, so tired of arguing. "Not you too."

"I've said my piece," she said, holding her hand over her chest. "You are free to make just as many mistakes as the rest of us are. I just think this one is the one you'll regret for the rest of your life."

"Thanks for the pep talk," I said, giving her a thumbs-up

"Speaking of Mr. Biggest Regret of Your Life," she said, smiling sweetly at me, "where is the arch-nemesis screwer?"

I lifted a shoulder. "Heading back to school," I guessed.

"How?" she asked, looking over at me like I was making a joke.

"With his POS truck that gets two miles to the gallon and has an impressive array of fist dents dotting the bed." And she had the nerve to call me daft.

"That POS was towed two nights ago, after he showed up," she said, standing up and walking toward the window. "One of the guys who hung around all weekend said Jude drove that truck right up to the front door and left it there while he searched every floor and room for you. I guess the school decided a truck blocking the front entrance of one of their dorms was a parking violation."

"So how's he getting back?"

"Unless there's a bus line that runs from New York to Syracuse late on a Sunday night, I'd say he's hoofing it," India replied, peering out the window.

"You've got to be kidding me," I muttered, knowing she was right. Jude was just crazy enough to attempt it. Or he'd wind up hitching, and the thought of the kind of person who might pick him up made my stomach jump into my throat.

"India," I said, hopping up, "will you find him and drive him home? Please?" I wasn't above begging.

"No can do, chicky-dee," she said, plopping into her chair and firing up her laptop. "I've got more homework tonight than a Latin man has mojo."

"India," I whined, giving her a sad face that did nothing but earn an eye roll from her.

"Sorry, I can't do it," she said, fishing something out of the pocket of her hip-hugger jeans. "But you can use my sweet-ass car. She'll get you there faster and safer than your Mazda." Tossing the keys at me, she waved me away. "Now be off with you. He can't be more than a couple miles."

Looking up at me, she smirked. "Two down, only about another two hundred and fifty to go."

Glaring at her, I grabbed my purse and marched toward the door.

"Have a nice trip," she called after me, purring like a minx.

Making my way back down the hall, down the stairwell, and out the door, I debated taking India's car over mine. As soon as I stepped into the cold November night, I decided. Heated leather seats it was.

Once inside the garage, I trudged over to the luxury something-or-other. I glanced around, not really expecting to see Jude, but kind of hoping I would. I fumbled with the buttons on Indie's key, finally managing to get the thing unlocked on the third try. Sliding into the seat, I adjusted it forward because India was pushing six feet, turned the key over, and cranked the heated seats to the high setting.

Warmth drifted up my body almost immediately.

Pulling out of the garage, I decided to drive the route I drove every other weekend when I headed up to see Jude. I didn't know if he'd taken it—I didn't even know if he was on foot—but it was a starting point.

I cruised a few miles below the speed limit, whipping my head from sidewalk to sidewalk, sure I'd see him the next block down. The next block turned out to be three miles down the road. India had been right. He was planning on walking from New York to Syracuse on foot.

Not that I needed any more confirmation, but the man was crazy.

His walk was purposeful, his shoulders rolled forward and his hands stuffed into his pockets, trying to stay warm. I could see the fog from his breath as I approached him. I rolled down the window.

"Need a ride, cowboy?"

His mouth curved up as he continued down the sidewalk. "Girls shouldn't offer rides to crazy men roaming the streets late at night."

I reminded myself I was mad at him and that we were taking a break. After I gave him a lift home. "I like my men crazy."

Stopping, he turned and walked toward the car. "Then I'd love a ride," he said, sliding into the passenger seat and smiling over at me. It was the sad kind, though, because it didn't reach his eyes.

"Cold?" I asked, turning his seat to the high setting.

He lifted a shoulder. "I've been colder."

I could tell he was hiding something between the lines—like a subliminal message—but I wasn't sure what.

"Okay then," I said, hitting cruising speed. "Syracuse or bust?"

Hanging his hands in front of the heater, he looked away from me and stared out the window. "I'll take 'or bust.'"

I glanced over at him. The heat blasting through the car heightened Jude's normally subdued scent. Every breath I inhaled smelled of Jude. Every breath hurt. "Of course you would."

"You and I both know where I'd rather be, but since I can't have that, then sure, Syracuse will work."

I looked down at the clock glowing neon green in the dark. We'd ticked off a whole five minutes in what was a five-hour journey. If he kept throwing these kind of topic punches, I was going to be TKO before we hit the George Washington Bridge.

"Could we not do that?" I asked. "I need a break. You agreed to one. But I couldn't let you walk a million miles in the cold and dark. Can we just play nice?"

"Yeah, Luce," he said, tilting his head back on the seat

rest. "I can play however you want me to play."

By the time we were cruising up the Thruway, Jude and I hadn't said another word to each other. We'd never mastered the art of small talk, and since the heavy stuff was off the table, we settled into an agreed-upon silence. Although it didn't feel quiet.

At the first pit stop, Jude insisted that he drive, and those were the first and last words he said to me the rest of the way.

TWELVE

I jolted awake, but my jolt fizzled short. I was in the passenger seat of India's car, the seat belt tight around me, the morning light just starting to stream into the car. I was staring at the ceiling, since my seat was reclined. Unbuckling my belt, I shifted in my seat. We were parked outside of Jude's house.

Jude was reclined in the driver's seat, awake, and watching me.

"What time is it?" I asked, shifting farther onto my side to look at him straight on.

"A little after seven, I think," he said, and the crescents beneath his eyes darkened. I wasn't sure how long Jude had gone without sleep, but I knew whether it was one night or four nights, it was unhealthy.

I was as unhealthy for him as he was for me.

My first class was at eleven, so there was no way around being late unless I booked twenty miles over the speed limit. "I've got to get going," I said, reaching for the switch on the side of the seat to lift the seat back up.

Jude didn't move; he just stayed reclined, curled into that position, staring into the space I'd just been asleep in.

Finally, he sighed. "Yeah. I know."

Moving the seat up, he exited the car. He waited for me as I came around the front, holding the door open and toeing at the ground.

Another good-bye I had to say to Jude, the semipermanent kind, and I didn't want to do it again.

"Bye," I whispered, squeezing past him to crawl into the car. The word stuck in my throat, tasting acrid.

His arms suddenly wrapped around me and pulled me against him, surprising me. He held on to me, refusing to let me go, and I let him. In the past, Jude had always felt like the one holding me up when we were close like this, but now it felt like I was the one holding him up.

Nuzzling into my neck, his body shook once. I was going to start sobbing again if he didn't let me go.

I was one breath breathed against my neck away from dropping my first tear when his arms lifted away, feeling like he was breaking through concrete to free them.

"Bye, Luce," he whispered, pressing his lips into my

temple before turning around and heading into the house.

He didn't look back once, but I watched him the whole way until he'd disappeared into the house. Crawling into the car, I adjusted the driver's seat, and right before I pulled away, I glanced up into Jude's bedroom window. He was taking up the window, watching me with the same brooding expression he had as he walked away from me.

Why did I do this to myself? Why didn't I just put foot to pedal, not giving the window a second thought?

Of course I knew the answer to that. I loved him.

But sometimes, as I was learning, love just wasn't enough.

A few weeks went by. A few weeks had never passed so slowly.

Jude kept his word, giving me the space I needed, not so much as sending a "Hey" text my way. Because I was who I was, one part of me was thankful to him for following my request, and another part was hurt. But because Jude was who he was, nothing or nobody told him what to do, and a part of me knew that if he really wanted to text me, he would have.

The Thursday following our separation, I'd woken up to a new set of heavy-duty studs on the Mazda. There wasn't a note or anything that would indicate who was the overnight tire fairy, but of course I knew. I didn't know how he'd done it, but the gesture—knowing what they'd cost and the time it'd taken him to put them on—made me shed a fresh set of tears that morning after having a day's break.

The next week, I awoke to a rose propped up on the windshield. A red rose.

I'd been reduced to one of those emotional girls I rolled my eyes at, leaving puddles of tears everywhere I went. It pissed me off to no end, but I went with it. Going without Jude felt like going through life without a compass, so if my body needed some tears to help it cope, I could handle it. So I tried to lose myself on the dance floor. I threw myself into dance, what had always been my go-to therapy, and for the first time, it fell short in the healing department. No matter how long or how hard I danced, the pain never went away. It never even dulled.

Thomas and I had danced at the winter recital last weekend, and people were still talking about it. I'd refused to let myself look at the seat in the front and middle while we performed, because I knew if I found it empty or filled by someone else, I wouldn't be able to make it through the rest of the performance.

As Thomas and I took our bows, I caved, and my eyes drifted to that one seat that had been filled with a beaming face earlier in that year. Not tonight. A stone-faced middle-aged man sat in Jude's seat.

I had to cut the bowing and applause short, because I wasn't going to cry on stage.

I was a mess.

Friday afternoon, a week before school let out for winter break, I was hurrying toward my dorm, hoping the faster I walked, the warmer I'd stay against the not-quite-frigid temperatures. Dream on.

"I don't think you could look more pissed if you tried," a familiar voice called out as I walked up to the dorm.

Lifting my head, I found Tony propped on the top step in front of the door, burrowed in a big black hoodie and smiling his Tony grin at me.

"Long time no see," I said, letting myself smile. It felt good, having one piece of Jude close by.

Tony arched a black eyebrow. "Isn't that the way you wanted it?"

Wrapping my scarf around my neck, I walked up to him. "Damned if I know."

"You women," he said, shaking his head. "You play this tough game of pretending to know what you want, but as soon as we give it to you, you want the opposite."

I smirked at him as I climbed the stairs and swiped my card key.

"You're rather observant for a certified player," I said, holding the door open.

Hoisting himself up, Tony weaved through the door, and I followed behind him. He plopped into the first chair he came upon in the commons area. "These are some pretty nice digs," he said, appraising the room.

Taking the seat next to him, I slid my mittens off. "Why are you here, Tony?" I asked, because he had yet to mention it, and Tony and I had only been friends through Jude. We didn't have the relationship that would justify him driving five hours to visit me.

His face dropped. My stomach followed.

"Oh my God," I breathed. "Is Jude all right?" My mind, of course, started firing off a list of things that might have happened to him.

"What do you think?" he asked, eyeing me.

"Don't play with me, Tony," I warned, my heart starting to slow when I realized what Tony was getting at. Life and limb wise, Jude was fine. Heart and soul wise, he was a bloody mess, right along with me.

"In terms of your face-dropping reaction, yeah, he's fine. No broken bones, no dangling limbs, no fast-spreading tumors."

I waited for my pulse to return to normal. "So what's up?"

Looking at the floor, Tony leaned forward, propping his

elbows on his knees. His foot was tapping the floor like a piston on speed.

"I heard about what happened with Adriana," he began, causing me to flinch. I'd gone three weeks without hearing that name and trying not to think about it. Hearing it now slammed me up against a wall.

"I heard Jude's story, he told me your story, and Lord knows I had to hear Adriana bragging about how she's bedded the quarterback with a girlfriend."

I was wishing I hadn't invited Tony inside.

"Anyways, I didn't think much of it after the drama died down a bit. I believed Jude because he's my boy, but even I have to admit I had my doubts about the whole 'no way in hell would I or did I screw Adriana Vix' testimony," he said, his eyes moving around the room. "I mean, she's Adriana Vix. Adriana. Vix."

"I get it, Tony," I interrupted, not in the mood for him to get a hard-on while he fantasized about her in front of me. "What's your point?"

Shaking his head, he glanced over at me. "A couple nights ago, I was with my Spirit Sister, being"—his face lined as he contemplated how to put it—"*serviced*, and she might have been a tad tipsy and run her mouth a bit more than Adriana would have liked."

That was one sentence that I couldn't and didn't want to wrap my mind around. So I looked at Tony and waited.

"My Spirit Sister's Payton Presley," he explained, which didn't explain anything to me. "She and Adriana are, like, best friends. At least as much as girls like those two can be best friends. It's more like, 'You're my favorite enemy, so I'll drive the dagger into your back when you turn around.' That kind of thing."

None of this had to do with Jude and me.

"And?" I tried not to sound irritated.

"So Payton was running her mouth in bed about how at least she didn't have to stage a screw with her football player."

My heartbeat picked up pace again.

"I pressed her for more details, and apparently Adriana told her everything that happened. About Jude storming into the house after your fight, shutting himself in his room with a bottle of tequila. And so, don't hate me," he said, looking over at me like he was scared of me. He had me by a hundred and fifty pounds and he looked like he wanted to hide from me. "But I might have been the one to mention your and Jude's fight to Adriana that night. Jude gave me the rundown as to what had happened. Not much—he really didn't want to talk—but I didn't think it was that big of a deal telling her when she showed up late that night."

Everything was coming together now. And the realization of what had happened was making me sick to my stomach.

"Payton told me Adriana guessed that you would eventually come walking through that front door, so she camped out in Jude's room, stripped him down while he snoozed in a tequila stupor, and hung out in a bathrobe in front of the window until you pulled up." Tony sighed, leaning back into the chair and staring at the ceiling. "And you know the rest."

Words failed me. My heart beat so hard it was echoing through me. There were so many things I needed to say and I needed to do. Jude had told the truth.

He hadn't slept with Adriana. He'd told me it didn't matter how drunk he got, he never would want anyone but me. Or at least hadn't at the time. Who knows if he had changed during our weeks apart?

I had about a hundred questions for Tony, and about a million things I wanted to say, but only two words were on the tip of my tongue.

"That. Bitch."

Tony nodded. "Not exactly breaking news there, Lucy." Popping to a stand, he looked down at me. "I know this is none of my business, and I'm gonna catch a shitload of heat from the cheerleaders if they find out I ratted one of their own, but I don't care. I like Jude. I like you. He *loves* you," he said, shoving his hands in his pockets. "You deserve to know the truth."

I had known the truth for weeks now, and I'd refused to let it take root.

"Sorry to throw this all on you, Lucy. I know you wanted your space and time and everything, but I couldn't not tell you."

"Does Jude know you're here?" I asked, contemplating my next move.

"Nope," he said, giving me a sheepish smile. "And he'd probably kick my ass if he did know."

I nodded. He patted my leg before heading toward the door. "I gotta get back. We're throwing a huge bash at the place tonight, and someone's got to tap the kegs."

"Tony?" I called after him.

Stopping, he turned around.

"Thank you."

"What can I say?" he said, running his fingers through his dark hair. "I might never find something as special as what you guys have together, but I sure as hell am not going to let you guys throw it all away."

Was that what everyone thought I'd done? Thrown Jude's and my relationship away? That was nowhere near how I would have described it. If anything, I carried it with me everywhere I went.

"Talk to ya later, Lucy," he said, waving before throwing the door open and leaping down the stairs.

Later wasn't going to be all that far off, I decided.

Going with my gut, letting it dictate something that was rash and every shade of spontaneous, I burst out of the room and was bouncing down the front stairs of the dorm as Tony's truck peeled down the street.

A few minutes later, I hopped into my car, heading out of the parking lot with only one person's face on my mind as I headed north.

THIRTEEN

double cappuccino, one pit stop, and half a tank of gas later, I was pulling onto the street Jude's house was on. The street was full of cars, but I didn't let that stop me. I had a one-track mind, and now that I was close to putting my plan into action, I rolled up in front of the house, put the car in park, and left it smack in the middle of the street. Jude's truck was back in the driveway. Good. If my car got towed, I knew how I'd get it back.

Bounding across the yard and up the stairs, I let myself inside. It didn't sting as bad as I'd thought it would, being here after weeks of separation, but I knew that had everything to do with the adrenaline that was firing to life right now. I had a message to deliver, and I wasn't leaving here until Jude heard it.

I weaved through the room crammed with bodies. I slid out of my coat and dropped it on the closest piece of furniture. My hat and mittens followed. I recognized a few faces in the crowd, but most were strangers who were probably wondering what had put the furious expression on my face.

I made my way to the end of the room. Jude was sitting on the couch, alone, a full cup of beer in his hand, staring into the fireplace where no fire burned. His gray beanie was sitting low on his forehead, and he was wearing the leather jacket I'd gotten him.

My stomach ached when I saw him like this. I wanted to wrap my arms around him and melt the statue back into the man I loved.

But that would have to wait.

I'd come here looking for someone else.

I'd driven five hours to find that bitch Adriana Vix and give her a piece of my mind—my fist doing the giving.

I didn't have to guess who was in the center of the circle of guys over by the dining room table. A fresh burst of adrenaline shot through me as I marched across the room. I shouldered and shoved my way through the guys, squaring myself in front of Adriana.

For one second she looked surprised to see me; then her eyes narrowed. She crossed her arms, looking put out that I was taking up her space.

"What?" she said, tilting her head.

I grinned. She shouldn't have come at me with words when I was way past words. My arm was already swinging back when her eyes widened, realizing I wasn't in the "talking" mood.

My fist clocked her across the cheek, throwing her back into the crowd of shock-faced guys.

"That's what!" I said, shaking my hand. Those cheekbones of hers were sharp, but damn if it wasn't worth it. "Bitch!" I tacked on, glowering at her.

Adjusting herself, she swatted away the guys who were fussing over her. Those green eyes of hers swirled black.

"You're going to pay for that," she seethed, her fists clenching. "That's gonna leave a bruise."

Without so much as a second thought, my other arm shot across my body, landing on the other side of her face. "There!" I shouted, shaking that hand too. "Have another so they'll match."

Adriana's bronze skin flashed red right before she came at me, her fingers wrapping around my neck. "You overrated whore!"

Driving me into the table, her fingernails digging into my neck, she kicked my legs out from underneath me. My back slammed into the table, the air immediately rushing from my lungs.

The impact had loosened her hands, so I shoved myself down the table, but not before grabbing a handful of her hair and pulling it along with me.

Adriana screamed, sounding like a constipated lioness. She lunged across the table at me and scratched my arm. Holy Freddy Krueger nails. Those were going to leave a scar.

As Adriana and I wrestled and rolled, a crowd was gathering around the table. Guys were hollering, throwing their fists in the air, chanting, "Catfight. Catfight. Cat. Fight!" We were giving them the catfight of the century.

Adriana's slut-length dress had inched its way up over her ass cheeks, and the thong she was wearing left nothing to the imagination. I had at least come prepared to do battle. I was wearing a pair of jeans, but somewhere along the way, Adriana had torn my blouse down to my navel, so my white-lace-covered tits were on display to all the bulging eyes and raised cell phones.

Another hair-flying, palm-slapping roll down the table and I landed on top of Adriana, managing to pin her to the table with my legs. She squirmed beneath me, trying to free herself. This chick might have half a foot on me and ten pounds—if only in her bra—but I was a dancer, and I could strangle a rhinoceros with my inner thighs if I needed to.

Raising my hand in the air, I slapped it down across her cheek.

"That was for all the other girls you've preyed on!" I shouted above her, folding my hand into a fist and bringing it back down. "And this one's for Jude." Her lower lip was split and bleeding, her cheeks dotted red from countless slaps and hits, and her hair looked like a hurricane had just come to town. I couldn't have looked much better.

"And this is for me," I said, gulping in a breath and raising my middle finger at her. I smiled down at her, keeping my finger hanging above her face.

Shrieking, she squirmed harder, managing to get a leg free, which she promptly bucked right onto my chin.

I flew off the table, landing on the floor at the feet of countless spectators. Adriana leaped off the table, landing on top of me, unleashing a frenzy of hits and grunts. This couldn't even be classified as a catfight anymore. In fact, I was sure once this whole thing went viral, the WW-something would be calling us to sign wrestling contracts.

"What the hell!" a voice shouted above the din. Before Adriana could land another fist into my face, she was shoved away, landing on her butt-flossed ass a few feet away.

"Luce," he breathed outside my ear, sounding as scared as I'd ever heard him. "I've got you." Two strong arms looped around me, lifting me gently to his chest. "What the hell were you doing? Are you okay?" he asked, swallowing when he looked down at my face.

"Did I win?" I asked, letting him tuck me closer to him.

He glanced down at Adriana, his eyes narrowing.

"You kicked ass, baby," he said, one corner of his mouth lifting as he looked down at me.

The pain started hitting me then, spreading from my head.

"Then I'm all right," I replied.

Exhaling, Jude shook his head. "Let's get you out of here, killer," he said, steering me through the crowd, not caring who or how many people he bulled over.

"You slut!" I shouted down at Adriana for good measure.

She wiped her bleeding lip and sneered up at me. "Even on my worst day, your boyfriend still jerks off to my face when you're not around."

This bitch wouldn't take a hint. I squirmed in Jude's arms, trying to free myself so I could finish what I'd started. He only held me tighter.

"Ready for round two?" I seethed at Adriana, shoving against Jude's chest.

"Lucy," he said, moving through the crowd faster, putting more space between Adriana and me. "Calm down. Take a breath," he coached, looking into my eyes. One of them felt like it might have been swelling shut.

It took tremendous effort, but I did as he asked. I took a deep breath and visualized myself melting into his arms.

"And I thought I was the one with anger issues," he said, climbing the stairs. "I'm afraid after tonight, you've got me beat, Luce."

The pain was really starting to hit home now, pooling into every nerve ending.

"Anger through osmosis," I replied, moving my jaw. Yeah, that was going to bruise too.

I regretted the words immediately. His face fell, although he tried to keep his eyes from following.

I couldn't imagine how to rectify all the wrongs I'd thrown at Jude—I just seemed to keep adding more to the pile—so I folded my hand over his heart and let him carry me into his bedroom.

He walked me over to his bed, propping me in front of a mound of pillows.

"God, Luce," he said, kneeling beside me and examining my face. I didn't really want to know, and I sure as hell wouldn't be looking in a mirror for the next couple of weeks. "What the hell were you thinking?"

Running my fingers over my face, I winced at almost every place I touched. "I was thinking about giving that bitch a taste of her own medicine," I said, "my fist doing the dosing."

He exhaled, running his hand down the side of my neck.

"Don't worry," he said as I pulled my hands away to find blood spotting my fingers. "I'll fix you." He rose and headed across the room. "I'll be right back," he said, disappearing behind the door.

With Jude gone, the pain really started to eat away at me. I'd felt pain, and I wasn't a huge wuss, but this felt like every nerve had decided to grow a heart that was pounding.

It had felt so good at the time—giving and taking a beating with Adriana—but now I was starting to question why I'd done it. I wasn't regretting it, just questioning it. I'd never been a violent person. I had a short fuse, sure—but I'd never let my fists do the talking.

Why had I done it this time?

All the questions led to one answer: Jude.

He hadn't made me go after Adriana, but my love for him and the pain I'd experienced at Adriana's hands had been the fuel to my fire. I realized then it wasn't Jude who was the problem. He wasn't the reason our relationship was nothing short of explosive. It was me. It was the person I became when Jude was beside me.

My anger peaked at new levels, exceeding his, but I didn't have the self-control to douse that anger before it burned someone.

I couldn't fix us until I fixed me. And he couldn't fix me

for me. It was a task that was all my own.

It was one I wasn't sure I could face.

Jude was slipping back into the room before I could follow those thoughts down their depressing trail.

"Miss me?" he said, an armful of items tucked to his chest.

"Missed you," I answered, dropping my head back into the pillows.

"Lucky for you, Luce, you chose to pick a fight around me," he said, dropping the contents in his arms on the bed. "Someone who's patched up, attended to, and sewn shut just about any wound man or woman"—he smirked over at me—"could inflict on one's body."

"I had it all planned out," I said as he doused some cotton pads with alcohol. "Did you really think that was a in-the-heat-of-the moment I-really-should-have-known-better smack-down?"

"Oh, no, Luce. That looked like you knew exactly what you were doing."

Dabbing my cheek with the cotton, he flinched before I did. It stung, but no worse than any other part of my body.

"You're getting to be a worse liar with each passing day," I said, wincing when he ran the pad over my eyebrow. Must have earned myself a nice little gash there.

He grinned at my eyebrow. "Truth through osmosis."

I started to smirk at him, but it hurt my face too much, so I settled for a small glare. He ignored it, continuing to wipe my face meticulously.

I shouldn't have, but I watched him working over me, his eyes narrowed in their focus, the tip of his tongue bitten between his teeth, as he attended to every scratch, bruise, and cut. I'd never experienced hands as gentle as his were.

"Do I look like a mummy yet?" I asked a while later, when he leaned back and investigated my face after slipping another bandage into place.

"Nah," he said, capping the tube of first aid ointment. "You look like the most beautiful badass I've ever seen."

"High praise coming from the king of badass," I said, smiling through the pain it caused to move my mouth.

Collecting up the empty wrappers and bloodstained cotton pads, he dumped them into the garbage can. "Mind telling me what that was all about?"

"I told you," I said. "Giving Adriana Vix a piece of Adriana Vix."

"Yeah," he said, dragging out the word. "But you've wanted to stick it to Adriana since the night dumb-ass Tony mentioned her. Why did you choose to do it tonight?" Shaking a bottle of pain relievers into his palm, he handed me three tablets. I swallowed them down without any liquid.

"Because 'dumb-ass Tony' paid me a little visit earlier

today that triggered the need-to-throw-down-Adriana trap."

Jude studied my hands folded on my lap. "He told you what Payton told him?"

"Yeah."

"So was it me or Tony who convinced you I was telling the truth?" The wrinkles around his eyes deepened.

"You, Jude," I answered. "I promised you I'd trust you. I didn't want to believe it, but I trusted you. Tony was just the one who shone a light on the truth."

His jaw tightened. "So when you got in your car and drove here, were you coming to see Adriana? Or me?"

I couldn't lie to him, but I couldn't verbalize the truth. My lack of response answered his question.

His eyes closed as his head fell into his hands.

"Jude," I began, "no matter who I came here to see, I didn't come here to hurt you." Sliding down the bed, I wished the pain relievers would kick in faster. "The last thing I want to do is hurt you. And that's all I seem to be capable of lately."

The only solution to keep from hurting him anymore was to leave.

"Thanks for the patching up," I said, scooting off the end of the bed. "You really do know what you're doing when it comes to fight wounds. Lucky me." I flashed him a smile over my shoulder as I stood up. I staggered in place as every muscle screamed from the movement. Gritting my teeth, I headed toward the door.

"Do you really hate being around me so much now that you'd hightail it away from me when you can barely stand?"

His words stopped me, but it was his voice that broke me. That deep, warm voice a girl could lose herself in had just been drained of all its soul.

"I don't hate you, Jude," I said, staring at the door. "I love you. That's the problem. I love you so damn much it's unhealthy." I caught a sob that was about to burst from my chest. "That's why I needed time and space. That's why I can't stay here with you a minute longer."

"You've had time, Luce. I've given you your space," he said, the bed moaning as he stood. "I've aged fifty years in three weeks' time because I did my part and stayed away from you. But now you're here. And maybe you're not here because of me, but either way, you couldn't stay away."

He paused, and while I didn't see what was playing out on his face because I couldn't turn around and face him, I could imagine.

"You need more time? Fine. I can do that. I could do anything for you, Luce. But please, for God's sake, just give me some hope."

A tear fell down my cheek, bleeding into one of my bandages.

"Give me the smallest sliver of hope there's still going to be a place for you and me on the other side of this."

I couldn't lie to him. I couldn't hurt him. Why these two desires couldn't fit hand in hand was one of the reasons I'd concluded life wasn't fair.

"I won't lie to you, Jude," I whispered, choosing not to lie to him, which, by admission, made me hurt him.

Now I really couldn't stay in this room any longer. I continued toward the door, my legs feeling like they were going to cave under me with each step. I bit back the tears.

"Don't go," he whispered.

His request worked on me like it had been a demand.

I heard the floor groan as he walked over it, slowly coming up behind me.

"Stay," he asked, stopping behind me. I could feel the warmth rolling from his chest, he was so close.

"I can't," I said, focusing on the shiny brass of the door-knob. It was both the gateway to my escape as well the path to my personal hell.

"I know," he said, the floorboards whining as he took one more step toward me. His chest ran against my back, but he didn't touch me anywhere else. "Don't stay because *you* want to. Stay because *I* want you to."

Dammit. My heart couldn't break one more time before it became impossible to put it back together.

"Come on," he pleaded, "think of it as an early Christmas present."

I closed my eyes.

"I know I'm not entitled to one, but I want one. I need one." Jude had just enough pride not to beg, but it was the closest I'd heard him come to it. "Stay."

And that was my undoing. The boy who made mothers cross the streets with their children when they saw him walking down the sidewalk; the boy who didn't have anyone else; the boy I loved, begging me as only he knew how to stay with him.

"Okay," I said, reaching my hand for his.

His fingers laced through mine, kneading them like they were capable of giving him strength. Turning me around, he lifted his hand to my face and looked into my eyes.

He let out the breath he'd been holding captive and folded me into his arms. Jude Ryder hugged me. He hugged me like I was everything he wanted and everything he could never have. He hugged me without the expectation of one embrace leading to something else.

It was the most intimate moment we'd shared. Fully clothed, vertically aligned, mouths separated, I was drowning in intimacy.

As his arms started to unwind from me, I grabbed one of his hands and led him to the bed. Lying down, I patted the space next to me. He crawled into it, the mattress rolling me around as he settled beside me. Winding my arms around him, I tucked my chin over his head, knowing in the morning, I'd have to let him go. But not now. Not tonight.

It made me wish that tomorrow would never come.

"I love you, Luce," he whispered, sounding like sleep was going to find him in the next breath.

I swallowed, pushing down the pain rising in my throat. "I love you, Jude."

I hadn't slept in weeks. Three weeks to be exact. Of course I knew what, or who, was responsible. Jude lay in the exact same position he had fallen asleep in last night, except the worry lines had disappeared from his face.

I was about to kiss those parted lips, but I caught myself in time.

I slid my arm from beneath him and rolled to the side of the bed. My body was stiff, like I needed to lubricate my joints to get them to move properly. I glanced over at Jude to make sure he hadn't startled awake, then slipped my boots on and stood up.

This feat hurt worse than it had last night. I prayed I still had that trial-sized bottle of pain relievers in the glove box. I let myself look down at Jude once more. I gave myself to the count of three. This was how I would choose to remember him when my heart ached with every beat after I left him. At peace, content as I slipped out of his life.

I turned away. I slowly moved across the room as quietly as a stiff-jointed person could. The door whined open, and my adrenaline spiked as I looked back at Jude, sure he'd be bursting awake.

But he was asleep, enjoying a few more minutes of peace before he woke up and found I'd slipped out on him without a good-bye. But maybe that was what last night had been. A good-bye.

Our good-bye.

Once I was down the hall, the stairs presented a challenge, as each step made me feel like the sore muscles in my legs were going to collapse. A few party stragglers decorated the couches and carpet, but once I made it past them, I was home free.

The Mazda hadn't been towed, beyond every miracle of traffic cops everywhere. I slid inside the driver's seat, turned the key over, and hit the gas the next instant. Now that I'd succumbed to the inevitable, I couldn't get out of here fast enough.

It was a couple of miles down the road, when I had my first red stoplight, that a folded piece of paper resting on my dash caught my attention. I kept my car clean, almost anally clean, so I knew it couldn't have been some random outline or class notes. Grabbing it, I unfolded it, immediately recognizing the handwriting.

> *I just wanted you to know I'd be chasing after you right now, naked if need be. But because I'm respecting your request for time and space, I'll force myself to lie here in bed and pretend I'm asleep.*

It wasn't signed, but it didn't need to be. Jude knew I'd leave him without a proper good-bye. Sometime in the night, he'd woken up to scribble down a note and tuck it inside my car. Knowing this made me curse the day I'd let doubt enter my life, the doubt that had wedged its way between me and Jude until it had built a wall so high there was no way I could see to scale it.

I kept the note in my lap the entire drive home.

FOURTEEN

chool was officially out for winter break. The dorm had been all but vacant as of last night. India had left for a sunny and sandy Christmas in Barbados, and since my flight wasn't until Sunday morning, I was going to have a quiet weekend all to myself. The prospect wasn't appealing on any level of the pleasure scale.

Other than the note, I hadn't had any contact with Jude. And even though I'd cried in my bed every night since, feeling his phantom arms around me, it had been worth having eight hours with Jude Saturday night. That pleasure then was worth that pain now.

I sat in the swivel chair, watching the coffeepot percolate, still winding down from my early-morning dance session. I knew I couldn't bear to hang out in this empty room for another twenty-four hours. Rushing to my closet before I could change my mind, I slid into a pair of leggings and my boots, and debated what top to wear. The debate was over when my hand clutched the ginormous orange sweatshirt folded on the top shelf. I pulled it on, and after rearranging my hair and dabbing on a few smears of makeup, I was out the door, my keys and purse in hand.

I got in the car and headed north, checking the fuel indicator to make sure I had a full tank. It was going to be a long drive.

Today was a big play-off game for Syracuse. A day-before-Christmas-Eve game that was expected to be the game of the season. I couldn't miss it. I'd already missed Jude's last couple of home games thanks to our monthlong "break," and I couldn't bear to miss another.

We might have been taking a break, but I could still fade into the crowd of tens of thousands and enjoy seeing him play the game that seemed created for him. I justified doing a selfish thing since I was alone just before Christmas.

I passed the drive listening to tunes and trying not to think about Jude, failing, and then giving myself an early Christmas present and allowing myself to think about Jude as much as I wanted to today.

It was less than a half hour to kickoff, which meant I had to park a mile away and trek in. I loved a football game—I always had. Even as a toddler plucking grass on the sidelines at my brother's games, I'd loved it.

I loved the roar of the fans, I loved the clash of helmet hitting helmet, I loved the energy in the air, I loved the smell of hot dogs. I loved it all.

But most of all, I loved watching Jude play. He played with the heart of a dancer who truly loved the game. He would have played every day even if it wasn't in exchange for a college scholarship, or one day, I bet, in exchange for millions of dollars a year in the NFL.

Jude played because he loved it.

And I loved watching him play.

Making my way up to the ticket window, I immediately wished I would have picked another.

"If you don't just get prettier every time I see you, young lady," the elderly man behind the window said with a smile. His name was Lou, and he reminded me of my grandpa. "I haven't seen you the past couple games. Mr. Jude hasn't been messing things up with you, has he now?"

I smiled back politely. "No, Mr. Jude hasn't been doing anything to mess things up," I said, folding my arms over the counter.

"That's good to hear, Miss Lucy. I wouldn't want to have to teach him a lesson on how a man's supposed to treat a woman."

"I don't think any of us would want that." I smiled and

waited for Lou to wrap it up. The old man loved bantering back and forth with me, and I was usually happy to play along, but this time was different. I doubted that if he knew how I'd hurt Jude, he'd be teasing me good-naturedly now.

Skimming through the stack of tickets, he pulled out two. Jude always left one for me and an extra in case I wanted to bring a friend. "I was wondering if these tickets would go unclaimed again today," he said, sliding them through the window. "If I wasn't certain Mr. Jude would have marched off the field to physically remove me, I might have slipped into one of these seats."

"Why don't you take them today, Lou?" I said, pushing them back toward him. "I just want a general admission ticket today."

"Why would you want a general admission when you've got front-row seats on the fifty, honey?" The frown lines deepened on his face.

"Please, Lou?" I asked, biting my lip. I didn't want to explain to him what I couldn't quite explain to myself. "Just one general admission ticket?"

He sighed, tapping his fingers over the counter. "Okay," he said, "but only because I can't say no to a pretty face."

Stacking a GA ticket on the other two Jude set aside for me every game, he slid them back through the window at me. "It's on the house, but you have to take these two with you. Mr. Jude would have my job if he found out you were here and I didn't at least give them to you."

"Thanks, Lou," I said, taking the tickets. "Maybe one of these games you and I can use these together."

Lou's brown eyes softened. "That would be a real honor, Miss Lucy."

I waved to Lou, then headed for the gates. "Thanks again."

He nodded, at a loss for words.

The roar of the crowd amplified as I approached the stands. Syracuse was taking the field. I hurried, not wanting to miss it. This was one of my favorite moments of the game. When Jude came sprinting onto the field, leading an army of men, all of them looking like they were as invincible as they believed they were, I got goose bumps every time.

Jude was only at the twenty when I made it within view of the field. Right as I watched him charge the field with his teammates, I knew I'd made the right decision in coming. The weight I'd had strapped to my back broke loose the moment my eyes found him. I could fill my lungs again, I could form a smile that didn't feel forced, I could feel my heart beat like it wasn't a chore anymore.

I stared at him until the team settled into pregame warm-up before making my way to my seat. I also might have spied a certain cheerleader with bruises on both cheeks.

Unlike mine, her battle wounds weren't mostly concealed by foundation. It felt good knowing I packed a more powerful punch than the Queen of Mean. Realizing I'd wasted enough energy on Adriana Vix, I headed to my seat. I squeezed by a very pregnant woman and a guy dressed in an army uniform, who I assumed was her husband. I glanced back at them again. They inspected their tickets, then gazed up into the stands. She slowly took the first step up.

I stopped, watching her take a second step. If being pregnant meant taking five seconds to climb one step, I wasn't sure I'd enjoy it very much.

"Wanna trade?" I asked suddenly. I couldn't watch her suck in another breath as she attempted another step. "They're pretty good seats."

The husband looked at me, confused, then studied the tickets I was holding out for them. His eyes widened.

"Don't get me wrong, miss, because I'd sell my first-born for tickets like these"—he shot his wife a sly smile as she smacked his arm—"but see that row, way in the back? Those nosebleeds are our seats."

I liked these two already. "How's the view from up there?"

"It sucks," he answered, helping his wife down the two stairs she'd just scaled.

Shoving the tickets into his hand, I smiled. "Well, the

view from these seats doesn't," I said, backing away.

Kickoff wasn't going to wait for me to get my butt into my seat. "Just do me a favor and make sure to give number seventeen a hard time." Turning around, I kept walking, smiling the whole way to my seat.

Lou had scored me a solid general admission ticket. There were two empty seats at the end of the row; mine was the second one in. I smiled at the family in the row in front of me. When the littlest boy turned, I saw that he was wearing an orange number seventeen jersey.

"I like your shirt," I said. "I've got one just like it."

His eyes widened. It was good to know I could impress a five-year-old boy. "I want to be just like Jude when I grow up."

This boy had a smattering of freckles and a cowlick, and he was going to make me cry. For the damn hundredth time this past month.

"Me too," I said as he swung around in his seat.

His mom threw me an apologetic look. I waved it off. "I shouldn't be telling you this, since you're a stranger *and* a girl, but Jude's a superhero in disguise," he whispered.

"He is?" I said, glancing down at Jude on the field, warming his arm up. Tossing the ball, he glanced over to the stands, studying the front row. "Doesn't the orange-and-white spandex kind of give his superhero status away?"

The boy's face scrunched up as he puzzled over that one. Two seconds later it cleared. "No," he said with confidence. "Anyone can go out and buy some orange-and-white spandex. But no one else can be like Jude Ryder."

Pulling a pack of Red Vines from my bag, I offered him one. It was the least I could do for Jude's number two fan.

"Since I'm a girl and all, and am not up-to-date with the superhero circle," I said, grabbing my own piece of licorice, "what puts him in cahoots with the likes of Superman and the Wolverine?"

"Danny, are you bothering this lady?" his mom called across the row of what I guessed were his older siblings.

He shrugged. "I don't know," he said, looking at me. "Am I bothering you?"

"He's fine," I called down to his mom. "We're talking about one of my favorite subjects. Football." *And Jude.*

"Okay," she said, giving Danny the mom look. "Manners, okay?"

"K, Mom," he answered, propping up on his knees and sticking his chin on the back of the seat. "Your dad and mom haven't explained it to you yet?" he asked, his freckled nose wrinkling.

"Explained what to me?"

"Superheroes aren't real," he said, looking a little sad for me. "They're make-believe."

"But I thought you just said Jude was one," I said, chewing the end of my licorice.

The boy rolled his eyes and sighed. *"Comic book* superheroes aren't real. Jude's a real-life superhero."

"Ohhhh," I said, nodding my head. "I get it now."

Danny's head spun around as the teams lined up on the field for kickoff.

"So what qualifies Jude as a superhero?" I said, leaning forward. The visiting team kicked off as Syracuse charged down the field.

Danny shook his head at me, looking like this question was my most insulting one yet. "He's strong, he's fast," he began, counting items off on his fingers. "He can throw a football, like, ten miles. He's going to marry the most beautiful girl in the world, and they're going to make little superhero babies." He paused; I wasn't sure if it was because he was done with his list or catching his breath.

"Anything else?"

"And one day, he's going to be president of the United States of America," he said, twisting back in his seat as Jude led his offensive line into position at the sixty.

"So all those things make him a superhero, huh?" I said, continuing to make conversation. Partly because the kid could keep pace with me on a couple of my favorite topics: football and Jude. And secondly, because it felt good to talk.

To someone. Even if that someone was a pint-size, freckle-faced, superhero worshipper.

"Well, yeah, that and . . ." He stared down at the field as Jude pulled one of his notorious quarterback fakes and ran that ball into the end zone before the other team had figured out what the hell was going on. "That," Danny said, jumping in his seat and waving his hands toward where Jude had scored six points in the first minute of the game.

Once the cheering died down to a dull roar, Danny spun in his seat, grinning from ear to ear. "Now do you believe me?"

"I believe you."

And that was how the first half of the game continued. Danny and I would banter back and forth in between hollering our heads off when the home team got another ball into the end zone. I couldn't have imagined a better Christmas present for myself.

Like every game Jude had played, he played this one like his life was hanging in the balance. He was good because he had the talent. He was the best because he believed he was and played accordingly.

And every one of us in the stands recognized that we were witnessing a legend in the making. Jude's name wouldn't fizzle into college football record books; it would be eternalized by the young boys like Danny who would tell stories of Jude around the dinner table to their sons.

Maybe I was being sensitive, but it seemed as if Jude couldn't stop looking up into that front row whenever he was on the sidelines. I was probably just imagining it, hoping he was looking for me and wondering who the people were in my seats, but this was my Christmas present, and I had carte blanche to jump to whatever conclusion I wanted.

At the half, we were ahead by two touchdowns, an unreal feat given the analysts' prediction that this would be one of the closest games in college football history. I watched Jude lead the team off the field.

Once the game had kicked off, Danny had stayed mostly quiet other than throwing up football, or more specifically Jude, praises. I was about to hop up and grab myself some concessions when Danny started bouncing. He was looking way up, rows above us.

His eyes were popping out of his head. Then a bunch of other spectators started twisting in their seats, nudging their seatmates and pulling out their iPhones.

"Holy—"

"Danny!" his mom warned, shooting him a look. "Language."

I felt faint. I knew why. Jude was coming down the stairs.

"Hey, Luce," he said, stopping at the end of the row.

"Hi," I replied, giving him a sheepish smile. I hadn't

expected him to know I had come—I hadn't intended for him to ever find out.

"Enjoying the game from here?" he asked, dropping his helmet and sliding into the empty seat beside me.

"I am," I answered, not moving my arm now pressed against his on the armrest. "You're playing a great game. So much for everyone saying this might be the first game you could lose."

I could feel Danny's eyes on us, not missing a single thing. He really did believe Jude was a superhero, and he acted accordingly.

"Well, once I knew you were here, I might have kicked it up a notch," he said, smiling his tilted smile at me.

"Lou told you, didn't he?" I guessed.

"Lou didn't need to tell me, Luce," he said, looking between me and the field. "I don't need someone to tell me when my girl's in the stands. I could pick you out even if I was playing in the Superdome and you were tucked into the back row."

Of course he could. Couldn't I have done the same with him?

I was a fool to think I could pop into this game and pop out before he knew I was here. He knew I was here before I'd even known I was coming. That was the curse and the blessing of Jude's and my relationship.

"Aren't you supposed to be in the locker room, getting a pep talk from your coach? Maybe a second half action plan?" I knew Jude did what he wanted to, but I felt the need to remind him, since I couldn't have been squirming in my seat more from everyone around us watching us with unblinking interest.

"The plan is always the same," he answered, his eyes roaming over my face, likely inspecting the battle wounds from the catfight. "Kick. Ass."

"I think you've got that down," I said, knowing a few members of the visiting team could personally relate to that.

"What are you doing here, Luce?" he asked, still studying me.

"Watching you play," I answered, knowing it wasn't the answer he'd accept.

"Yeah," he said, making a face. "That's not going to work for me."

Of course it wasn't.

"You know why," I added with a whisper.

"I need to hear you say it," he said, swallowing. "I've gone too many weeks without hearing it."

Sighing, I closed my eyes. "I love you," I said, knowing

it was the truth and that it didn't change anything. "And I missed you."

"Yeah," he said, "me too."

Just then, the crowd, not just the people around us, took a collective gasp before unleashing a cheer that exploded through the stands.

"It's you guys!" Danny hollered, pointing at the huge screen across from us.

"Shit," Jude and I said in unison.

I was going to have the cameraman's head, because on that screen—as well as the other three around the stadium—was a close-up of Jude and me in real time, the red, bubbly KISS ME captions surrounded by floating hearts.

The stadium started chanting, "Kiss! Kiss! Kiss!" while my face went almost as red as those damn hearts floating around our faces on the screen. Jude wasn't red, though; he didn't even look uncomfortable. He was somewhere between a smile and a smirk.

If I hadn't known better, I would have believed he'd set the whole thing up.

I looked back at Jude.

His smirk was now a full-blown cocky, hot-as-hell smile.

"Get over here," he said, weaving his fingers through my hair.

I didn't have to do much "getting over here," because he

closed the entire space between us until his lips rested on mine. The crowd went wild—full-moon wild. Their hero didn't just kiss me. He consumed me.

His other hand lifted to my neck, his fingers curling into my skin, his lips urging mine, pressing them to respond.

I wasn't sure if it was feeling the eyes of thousands of fans on us, or the length of time that had passed since Jude and I had last kissed like this, or if it was the feelings that were washing over me—drowning me in their intensity—that terrified me. Jude was meant to be my one and only, had reality not gotten in the way and screwed everything.

Finally, he gave up. His lips stopped trying to work mine into submission. His fingers drooped against me, feeling suddenly cold.

The crowd was still buzzing, clueless that two hearts were breaking following that kiss.

"I've really lost you," he whispered, his words even cool against my skin. "You're gone for good this time, aren't you, Luce?"

I stared into those silver-gray eyes, not able to imagine anything I could do that was worse than hurting them.

"You can never lose me, Jude," I said, forgetting about the crowd. Forgetting about everything except every reason we should be together and every reason we couldn't.

"But I can't have you the way I want you," he said, running his thumb down my cheek.

"I don't know."

"Then what are you doing here, Luce?" he asked, his voice rising. "You want time? You want space? Fine. I gave that to you. But then you keep throwing yourself back into my life whenever the hell you choose. No warning. No apology. No permanence. You show up at my front door and sneak out the back without so much as a good-bye," he continued, never taking his eyes off me. "You couldn't take the up and down. The roller coaster was going to kill you. You know what I can't take? You in and out of my life before I even knew you were there in the first place. You looking at me the way you are now and then being able to turn your back and walk away five minutes later." His hand clenched over my cheek before he lowered it. "That is what will kill me. I can't live wondering if you're still mine to claim."

It was like he knew the exact words that could choke me up at the same time they'd fire me up. "I'm sorry," I said. "I just wanted to see you play one more time before I left for winter break. I never even thought you'd know I was here."

He snorted, curling his lip in disbelief.

"Fine. Me popping in and out of your life will kill you? Consider me officially done with popping."

"Will you knock that defensive, insecure girl shit out and

have an adult conversation?" he said, the muscles in his neck moving under the skin—a sure sign he was firing up too.

"Happily," I responded, gritting my teeth. "As soon as you do that can't-handle-the-pressure thing you boys do and get up and leave."

He paused, his face falling for one second before it fired back up. "You want me to leave?"

"I can't imagine anything that would make me merrier this holiday season."

"Fine," he said, shooting up. "I'll leave. But since you can't seem to stay away from me for more than a few hours, I'll see you soon, I'm sure."

"If by soon you mean never, then that sounds good to me," I replied, wanting to hop in my seat so I could get in his face. "Where do I sign?"

"You know, Luce?" he said, turning to head back up the stairs. "You have a shitty way of showing your love for someone."

I flinched. That one hurt more than I could remember words from other fights hurting me. Biting my lip, I glared at him.

"Right back at ya." And that was a bold-faced lie. Jude, perhaps more than anyone I'd ever known, was able to express his love as love was meant to be expressed.

Shaking his head at me, his face bled of all emotion before

he turned his back and jogged up the stairs. Clueless fans held out their hands as he ran by, but it was like he didn't see anything around him.

"Whoa," a stunned voice said, whistling a row below me. "You're the girl Jude Ryder's going to marry and make baby superheroes with?"

If Danny hadn't heard Jude's and my heated exchange, maybe that meant everyone within a ten-seat radius of me who were staring like I was a pariah hadn't either.

"I think I just lost any and all chance of that happening," I answered, feeling numb. Or at least, more numb.

"You are like the real-life Lois Lane," he continued, bouncing in his seat. "Only blonder. And younger. And prettier too."

I couldn't even make a halfhearted smile feel real.

He gaped at me like I was almost as cool as comic books. "Holy—"

"Danny!" his mom shouted, giving me a sympathetic smile.

So much for no one hearing.

FIFTEEN

*D*anny was watching me. Not saying anything, but something was eating this kid from the inside out.

"What is it, Danny?" I asked, tapping my foot anxiously.

"Why were you and Jude fighting?" he asked, looking relieved he'd gotten that off his chest.

"Because that's what we do, and we're good at it," I answered.

"But you love him?"

I glanced over at his mom, wishing she'd choose this time to usher the kiddos out for a bathroom break or something. "Yeah."

More relief flooded into his face. "So you're still going to get married?"

"I don't know," I said, biting my nails. Manicures were so last season. "I don't think so."

"Why not?"

"Because," I said, getting why parents were such a fan of this one-word-answer go-to. "Because sometimes love just isn't enough."

His freckled nose curled. "Well, duh," he said, flapping his hands over the back of the seat. "I just turned six and even I know that."

A six-year-old had more life wisdom, it appeared, than I did. The concept was more depressing than it should be.

"You know that, huh, smarty-pants?" I said.

"I know a lot."

"And as a kindergartener who's probably dated a total of zero girls," I said, arching a brow at him, "what exactly do you know about love?"

He did that little unamused face my mom had become a master of back in the day. "Mom told me that love is like a seed. You've got to plant it to grow. But that's not all. You need to water it. The sun needs to shine just enough, but not too much. The roots have to take hold," he continued, narrowing his eyes in concentration. "And from there, if it pops its head above the surface, there are about a million things that could kill it, so it takes a whole lot of luck too."

I felt my mouth ready to drop open. I was about to mutter

a curse when I caught myself. This kid was wise beyond his years.

"You can't plant a seed and hope it will grow on its own. It takes a lotta work to make anything grow." He smiled up at me, clearly pleased with himself.

"Wow," I replied, stunned. "That's some seriously smart stuff, Danny."

"I know," he said. "Do you have any questions?"

I was smirking at a six-year-old. Not one of my better moments. "I think I'm good, but I'll let you know."

He turned around in his seat, and I was halfway through a sigh of relief when he looked over his shoulder.

"You shouldn't have gotten into a fight with Jude," he said, his eyebrows drawn together. "You could really mess with his game. He might come back to the second half and be a mess. You might be solely responsible for losing the game if we do."

"Jude will be fine," I said, looking down on the empty field. "He's used to us fighting. It's never stopped him before."

He pursed his lips as he considered this. "That's sad," he responded. With the entire world of replies at his disposal, that was the one he chose.

"It is sad," I repeated as the stands started to explode with rising bodies and voices.

As Syracuse took the field after the half, Jude wasn't leading them. I almost panicked, sure our fight had unraveled him and he had taken off, never to be heard from again, but then I caught a glimpse of number seventeen in the middle of the pack.

I wasn't the only one who noticed. Confused, then accusatory faces turned my way. They might as well brand the word "pariah" over my forehead, because it couldn't have been any more uncomfortable than I felt now.

Kickoff was just getting under way when someone stopped at the end of my row. He was so obviously staring at me I couldn't even pretend I hadn't noticed.

"Yes?" I said in irritation, glancing up at the frat boy grinning down at me. His frat, Delta Delta Douche *Something,* was scrolled onto his baseball cap. I couldn't help rolling my eyes.

"This seat taken?" he asked, eyeing the empty seat Jude had occupied earlier. He'd sat in it for all of five minutes, but I was protective of it.

"Yeah," I said, dropping my purse onto it, "it is."

The crowd roared, cheering at whatever stellar play our kicking team had just pulled. Frat Boy was irritating me, smiling at me in a way that was way too cheesy and asking to occupy Jude's seat—he'd just made me miss the kickoff.

Strike Four. You're way the hell out.

"You better find another girl to sit next to." Danny turned in his seat, giving the stink eye to this guy who was three times as big as him. "This one is Jude Ryder's future wife."

"Hold up," the guy said, chuckling at Danny. "You're the QB's girl?"

Jude was just taking the field with his line when I saw him look my way. He was so far off it shouldn't have been possible, but I swore his eyes flashed black when he saw the guy lurking above me.

"Why don't you 'hold up' yourself and go back to the rest of your clan of future middle managers?" I said, scramming him away with my hand.

Snapping his fingers, the guy pulled out his phone and began thumbing through pages. I wasn't sure exactly what he was looking for, but I had a pretty good idea.

I watched Jude as he lined up, his head tilted back my way again. Damn it—he needed to focus on the game and not me. I could handle myself.

Frat boy's smile went Joker wide. "You *are* Ryder's girl," he said, flashing his phone at me. On the screen was a still of me straddling a crazed-faced Adriana, my arm high and my hair a tornado of white-blond wisps.

"I don't care if this seat is taken," he said, grabbing my purse and throwing it into my lap. "I need to get a picture with the girl who was on the winning side of the most-talked-about catfight in all college history." Wrapping his arm around me, he hung his phone out in front of us, about to take a picture.

When were asshats like this going to figure out they couldn't do whatever they wanted with a woman? We weren't beasts they could control. We were women who could rule the world with our eyes closed, but were smart enough to know to stay out of that whole mess. We were women—hear us roar.

And I did just that as I snatched his phone out of his hand, shot up in my seat, and hurled it down the stands.

Jude had just called the hike as my own projectile spiraled onto the sidelines. He took another look back at me when his eyes should have been nowhere but on the field. He froze when he saw what was taking place between me and Super Frat.

Jude watched me and I watched him, both of our faces lined with worry for each other. However, Jude's worry was misplaced. Frat Boy had selected a perfectly uncreative curse word to hurl at me before sulking away—back to his middle management hopefuls. But me, I had the right to an absolute gut-dropping worry, because breaking through Jude's offensive line, one of the visiting team's linemen barreled right for my frozen-in-place quarterback.

I was already screaming his name when the lineman drilled into Jude. Even after the initial impact, Jude's eyes didn't leave mine, but when his body crashed to the ground, bouncing and skidding a good ten yards, his eyes were long past the point of recognition as they fluttered closed.

"JUDE!" The scream was primal, coming out of some part of me I didn't know existed. I popped out of my seat and was running down the stairs before I knew I was running. My eyes were locked on him, his body contorted in a way that made my insides drop.

I wasn't thinking anything right then—I was all instinct. I blew by everyone in my path until I reached the concrete barrier separating the field from the stands and swung my legs over it.

I twisted onto my stomach so that I could curl over the wall and drop down to the field. The breath whooshed out of my lungs from the impact. I'd underestimated the drop, but it didn't slow me down.

Everyone was so focused on Jude and the trainers sprinting toward him, no one paid any attention to the crazed girl running down the field. I pushed and shoved by the players forming a circle around him and skidded to my knees beside him.

"Jude?" I cried.

The trio of trainers glanced up at me, eyes wide before narrowing. "You need to get the hell out of here, ma'am," one of them said as another removed Jude's helmet.

I let out one terrible sob and grabbed his hand. For the first time ever, it felt limp in mine.

"I'm not leaving," I replied, biting the side of my cheek.

"If you don't leave of your own accord, we'll have to have someone escort you out," the third trainer said, holding a light above Jude's eyes as he pried them open.

Another sob escaped. His gray eyes were flat, dead.

"I'm not leaving," I said, folding Jude's hand into both of mine, trying to infuse some warmth and life into it. "And I pity the person who *tries* to take me away from him." My eyes flashed.

"Fine," replied the one putting a brace around Jude's neck. "But you get in our way and I'll happily use the tranquilizer I keep in my case for emergencies on you. You understand?"

"Okay," I said. I wanted to heal Jude, running my hands over every part of him. It was a powerless feeling, not knowing what needed to be fixed.

One of the trainers plucked his phone from his pocket. "We've got to call this one in, guys," he said.

Biting the other side of my cheek, I stared at the spot on Jude's neck where the faintest movement could be detected. I started holding my breath, waiting for his pulse to kick in.

As long as he had a pulse, he was alive.

A couple more trainers ran onto the field, carrying a stretcher. The players moved away, hanging their heads as they wandered back to the sidelines. Moving the stretcher beside Jude, the trainers positioned themselves around him, sliding their hands into place.

I only let go of his hand so they could hoist him onto the stretcher. I clutched his hand as we made our way to the sidelines.

Maybe I was incapable of hearing anything due to shock, but the stadium went silent as we moved Jude off the field.

When we went through one of the team tunnels, I heard the blare of an ambulance siren. The paramedics were swinging the back doors open when we emerged. But when the words "concussion," "coma," and "paralyzed" were tossed out, I shut down.

As Jude was transferred into the ambulance, I followed behind the paramedic, taking a seat before I could be kicked out.

"Who are you?" he yelled over at me as the doors slammed shut.

"I'm the only family he's got," I whispered. I tried not to let the feeling that we were in a hearse on its way to a funeral cripple me.

We rushed into the emergency room. I watched helplessly as the person I loved was raced to the front of the line due to his injuries. Before everything that was happening could catch up with me, I was relegated to the waiting room.

To say that this didn't go over well with me would have been like saying it wouldn't have gone over well with Jude if our roles had been reversed. I went from Cursing, Crazy Woman to Sobbing Girl on Her Knees in the span of a minute. Psych unit, here I come.

Two security guards had to be called when I told a certain sour-faced nurse to go, *eh-hmm*, herself. They took one look at me, panicking and worried out of my mind, and let me off with a warning.

I paced the waiting room, fighting the urge at least one hundred times to shove past the security guard who'd clearly been instructed to keep an eye on me. My phone rang every minute with calls from Jude's teammates and friends.

I turned it off after ten minutes. What could I tell them? He'd been sequestered in an emergency room where more doctors kept rushing in than onto a golf course on a sunny Saturday morning? I didn't have any answers for how Jude was doing.

So I paced. I chewed my nails down to nothing. I ached in places I didn't realize could ache. But I wouldn't let myself contemplate the worst-case scenario. I was barely hanging on as it was.

It could have been fifteen minutes, it could have been fifteen hours, but when a serious-faced doctor finally breezed into the waiting room, it took a lifetime for him to cross the room toward me.

"I understand you're related somehow to Mr. Ryder," he said, folding his arms. He wasn't covered in blood, so I assured myself that was a good sign.

"Yes," I said, my voice hoarse. I was related to him in every way a person could be without the bond of blood.

"He's sustained a concussion from the impact," he began as my insides twisted. "I've put him into a medically induced coma to give his brain and body a chance to heal, but we won't know the full extent of the damage until he wakes."

I swallowed the bile rising in my throat. "He's all right?" My voice was barely a whisper.

"He's alive," the doctor corrected. "We won't know if he's all right until he wakes. Until then, he needs to take it easy and rest."

A nurse stuck her head around the corner. "Doctor," she interrupted, "we've got a car accident victim with internal bleeding coming in."

He nodded over his shoulder and started backing away.

"We've moved him up to the fifth floor. You can go see him now if you like."

"Thank you," I said as he rushed off. Words were inadequate when you were thanking the person who had saved the one you loved.

I followed the signs that led to the elevator and pressed the fifth-floor button. My legs were trembling, my breath was catching, my fingers were tapping over the elevator handrail. My anxiety was in such hyperdrive, the instant the doors whooshed open, I flew out and rushed toward the nurses' station.

"Excuse me?" I asked, my voice sounding as wired as the rest of my body felt. "Could you tell me which room Jude Ryder was taken to?" I didn't wait for the middle-aged, smile-wrinkled woman to look up from her chart before asking.

"He was just taken into 512," she said, pointing down the hall. "You can go see him right now. Just make sure he gets lots of quiet and rest, okay, hon?"

"Okay. I will," I said, wrapping my arms around my stomach. "The doctor said they put him into a coma so his brain could heal. Any idea when he'll wake up?" There were about a million questions I had now that I hadn't thought to ask the doctor.

"Could be next week," she said, with a shrug. "Could be

in the next hour. The brain is a tricky thing that's got a mind all its own." She smiled at her little pun. "The docs like to think they can command it to do their bidding, but in my experience, the brain wins every time."

Why couldn't all medical staff be as grounded as this lady? "Sounds very . . . inconclusive."

"Hon, whenever you're talking about the human body or brain, it's *always* inconclusive."

Not exactly what I needed to hear right now, but I'd take the hard truth over a warm, fuzzy lie most any day.

"Thanks," I said, waving as I headed down the hall.

"Let us know if you all need anything," she called after me.

Room 512 was at the far end of the hall, and the closer I got, the farther away the room seemed to get. This whole night had been a screwy version of *Alice in Wonderland*.

Sliding inside the room, I closed the door silently behind me. Looking at Jude on the bed, if I imagined it just right, I could pretend he was asleep in his own bed. But then the heart rate monitor beeped and the antiseptic smell of the hospital called me back to reality.

I didn't have an aversion to hospitals like most people did. To me, they were places where your loved ones who at least had a hope of being healed were taken. When my brother had been shot, the medical examiner's was the only place for him to go.

Jude was here, his heartbeat spiking and beating every second. That meant he was alive and had a fighting chance. There was hope.

I came around the foot of the bed and stared down at him. If it weren't for the hospital gown and wires and tubes snaking over his body, he would look like he didn't belong here. He didn't have any stitched wounds, black-and-blue bruises, or casts supporting broken bones. Everything on the surface looked perfect, but the true threat lay inside his brain.

I knew more about concussions than anyone who wasn't a doctor should. I had watched hundreds of football games in my lifetime, and I'd seen my fair share of boys knocked senseless. John had been lucky enough to escape the rite-of-passage concussion, but plenty of his teammates hadn't. Most recovered just fine. But some, the names and faces who were at the front of my mind now, were forever changed. Those poor guys would never walk onto a football field again, and a couple couldn't so much as lift a spoon to their mouths, let alone palm a football.

The realization that this was potentially what Jude would face made my entire body weaken. I shuffled along the side of his bed, then I collapsed onto the edge of it, grabbing his hand up in mine.

This was what happened when you didn't heed the

warnings life threw your way or listen to that voice in your head that told you someone was going to get hurt if you didn't stop fighting nature.

Jude and I had been riding a runaway train, and he was the one to take the brunt of the impact when that train crashed into the wall. I knew when and if Jude came out of this, we could try to piece things together, but it wouldn't be long before we'd hit another wall. And after falling apart once, we'd shatter with the next crash until finally, there would be nothing left of what he'd once been. There would be no Jude. No Lucy. No us. None of the love we'd shared. Just a mess that could never be fixed.

My hand was wringing the hell out of his, so I loosened my grip on him. The last thing he needed was a hand amputation after I'd cut off the circulation.

I knew I couldn't go, but I also knew I couldn't stay. And this cruel irony was the basis for Jude's and my time together. I loved him, but I shouldn't. I trusted him, but I didn't trust myself. I wanted him, but I couldn't have him.

With us, it wasn't like we were suffering from a bad case of wanting to have our cake and eat it too—we were just trying to make the best out of an empty cake plate. You couldn't create something out of nothing. Jude and I had the kind of something people spent their lives searching for, but life had given us a big nothing in the future department. If one of us didn't leave the other, all we could look forward to was having a meet-and-greet with death.

I knew it couldn't be him. Jude had warned me countless times before that he was incapable of walking away from me. So it had to me. I had to be the one to get up, turn my back on my man, and never stop walking away.

I'd never faced anything with so much fear.

Damn it. I was squeezing his hand all to hell again.

I cleared my throat; I tried to find the right words. Nothing. Something about acknowledging the permanence of my feelings kept the words bottled inside.

Good-bye. It would be the hardest thing I'd ever have to say, and the hardest thing I'd have to live. Jude wasn't just my first love. He was my forever love. But all the forces of nature were aligned against me actually being able to spend my life with Jude.

I was still choking on the word, when Jude's fingers flexed in my hand.

I jumped in my seat. Staring at his hand, I watched it come back to life, weaving through and around mine. Now something else was getting caught in my throat: relief.

His eyes flickered open the next instant, falling on where our hands were woven together. As I followed his gaze, I couldn't determine which fingers were his and which were mine. Another *Alice in Wonderland* moment, since his were rough, long man fingers and mine were skinny and soft all-girl fingers. Our hands had merged into one entity, creating its own Jude and Lucy. A Jucy or a Lude. The idea made me grin.

I felt his eyes move up, waiting for me to meet them. When I did, I wanted to set the world on fire and watch it burn for refusing to let me have this man.

His eyes grimaced with confusion as they scanned the room.

"You were hit, Jude. Hard," I explained, gripping his hand like centrifugal forces were trying to tear us apart. I didn't ease up because this time, his hand was gripping mine right back. "You blacked out and sustained a concussion, so the doctors put you into a coma so your brain could take its time recovering." So much for managing a coma. But it shouldn't have surprised me—Jude didn't conform to any standards, so a forced-on-him coma was no exception.

He cleared his throat. Then again, more forcefully. A wince pinched his face. I grabbed the pitcher of water from the cart and poured some in a cup. Lifting it to his lips, I held the back of his head while he took a few sips.

"I remember the hit," he said, reaching for his head. "The rest not so much."

"God, Jude. I'm sorry," I said, needing to say so much more.

"Sorry for what?" he said, inspecting the IV running into his arm. "That I was dumb enough to look in the opposite direction of a three-hundred-pound mamma-jamma who wanted to grind me into the Astroturf? That was all my bad, Luce."

"Yeah, but our fight," I said, scooting closer to him when I should be moving in the opposite direction. "You wouldn't have been so distracted if we hadn't just gotten into it."

"Luce. We fight. I'm used to that. Sure, that fight was the scariest-ass one we've ever had, but you're here now. That's all that matters. No matter how many fights we have, or how much they tip the Richter scale, none of it matters as long as at the end of the day, you're still with me."

He shifted in bed, propping himself up onto his elbows. "And I wasn't all that distracted by the fight. I was distracted by that d-bag I was planning to torture as soon as the game was done."

As he smirked at me, the color began to bleed back into his face. "That was one hell of a phone spiral you launched onto the field. I'm going to start calling you Laser Rocket Arm. If Coach saw that, he's going to dump my sorry ass and drop you into the starting QB spot."

I stroked his forearm, tracing patterns over the lines of muscle and vein. "If you keep taking hits like that, you'll be riding the bench for sure, Ryder."

He snorted. He didn't only think he was invincible, he *knew* it. Lifting his hand to his neck, he searched for something below his gown. His expression dropped. "Where the hell is my necklace?" he said, sitting up in bed and looking all over the room.

"I don't think you'll find it glued to the ceiling," I said when he investigated the white ceiling tiles.

"Where is it?" he asked, his voice tight.

"Jude," I said, worried he'd been hit too hard, "calm down. I'm sure it's around. They probably took it off when you were in the ER and have it tucked into a drawer or something. We'll find it."

"Okay," he said, exhaling, "you're right. We'll find it." Collapsing back onto the bed, he looked exhausted.

"Since when did you start wearing a necklace?" I asked, hoping it wasn't some huge gold chain with a hubcap-sized eagle hanging from it.

"Since I started trying to get my act together," he said.

"And that happened when?" I teased, narrowing my eyes at him.

He chuckled, that deep, throaty chuckle of his that went right through me, vibrating everything in its journey. As it tapered off, his face darkened.

"What?" I asked, ready to push that red button resting on the table beside the bed.

"I was dreaming," he said, his eyes going into that far-away place. "I remember it. That's what woke me up." One side of his face lifted higher. "It was the same dream over and over again. I must have had it a thousand times, and all I remember is wanting to break past that dream and wake up. But I couldn't. Something was holding me down. Something was keeping me from waking up."

That probably had something to do with a team of doctors putting him into a coma. A coma that had lasted all of an hour.

"What was it about?" I asked, wanting to reach inside him and extract all the poison that was eating him away.

His dark eyes flickered to mine. "You."

I swallowed. "Me?" I tried to sound brave, but I'd never sounded so scared. "What was I doing?"

I already knew his answer.

"You were leaving," he whispered. "You left me. And you never came back, no matter how hard I ran after you or how much I begged you to return." It could have been the drugs, or the horrible lighting in the hospital room, but for the first time, Jude's eyes looked like they could have spilled tears. "You left me."

And now it was my face and my everything else that was twisting as words failed me. It wasn't my head that reacted next; it was my heart. The heart that I had been depriving for so long had just busted free.

In an instant, I was straddling his lap, covering his mouth with mine. I kissed him, God, like I'd never kissed him before. I couldn't kiss him hard enough. I wanted his mouth to make me forget everything. I needed to forget reality for a while and pretend life was going to work out just the way I wanted it to.

His lips were quiet beneath mine as he processed what the hell had just happened, but when they came to, they moved against mine like they were trying to consume me right back.

The heart rate monitor started keeping beat to our frantic mouths retreating and advancing on one another. I ripped the sweatshirt over my head, and my tank was off and flying before the sweatshirt hit the floor.

Jude's hands grabbed my face, pulling me back to him, his tongue forcing its way into my mouth. I trembled, feeling his hands and his mouth and the rest of his body wanting, taking, and having me.

One hand crawled down my back, sparing no time in freeing my bra from my back. Now his breathing was almost as ragged as mine as we kissed each other. Realizing how weak and winded Jude was brought me back to reality. We shouldn't be doing this, for a baker's dozen of different reasons. And I didn't care about a single one of them right now. Reality wasn't the place I wanted to be.

His mouth moving in and over me wasn't enough to keep reality at bay.

I had to have all of him.

I took off everything that was still covering me, down my legs, around my ankles. Gone.

Jude's breathing hitched again as his eyes inspected me. Naked, tortured, and dying in my need for him.

"I'm one lucky bastard," he breathed, managing a smile as he propped himself up on his elbows. "And there's no way I'm letting anything get in the way of this"—his hands slid down my hips, curling into the flesh of my backside—"so help me get this damn hospital dress off."

I grinned, leaning down and letting my fingers work over the knots on the back of his gown while my mouth worked over the tendons and muscles of his neck. The beat of his heavy breath matched the beat of mine. I rose with him, I fell with him—always together.

Pulling the last tie free, I slid the gown up and over his arms. I threw it on top of my discarded clothes.

It was working. I felt nothing but the here and now. I felt nothing but Jude—his body, his love, and his need.

His hands returned to my backside, lifting it and sliding it back. I could feel him against me, waiting for my final acceptance, waiting to see if this was really the perfect

238

moment in time where Jude and I would finally take the last step of intimacy.

I was so ready, every nerve was throbbing. "You know your doctor said you were supposed to stay relaxed and rest," I said, smiling down on him, where his face was as excited as it was tortured. "I wouldn't say this counts as rest and relaxation."

His hands slid up my body, skimming up my breasts and molding beneath my jaw. As he held my face in his gentle hands, the lines and muscles of his face smoothed. "Luce. I love you. This is exactly what I need right now. Doctor's orders be damned."

My heart was pounding so hard in my chest, my sternum was starting to ache. This was it. The green light. Yet I also knew that a red light was on the horizon. I didn't want to acknowledge that red light; I wanted to pretend everything would work out and Jude and I could have the life we wanted. It was this land of pretend I found myself in as I lifted myself above him.

"*This?*" I replied, bracing my hands on his chest. His heart pushed against them.

He nodded, running his thumbs down my jaw. "This."

And then I lowered myself onto him, letting him consume me every way he could.

He groaned below me as his hands fell back to my hips.

"This?" I breathed, not able to catch it as I moved above him again.

We both winced from the separation.

His fingers curled into my hips, sliding them back down over him. The heart rate monitor was racing now, barely able to keep up with Jude.

"Damn this thing," he breathed, his forehead lining as I moved above him again. He ripped the wires from his chest, chucking them to the floor. His IV was next.

"There," he said, twisting below me, rolling me over until I was on my back beside him. "Nothing is coming between us," he said, nuzzling into my neck as he moved over me. I was vaguely aware the heart rate monitor was now beeping some sort of warning, but when Jude's hips rocked into mine, his moan getting lost inside me as he kissed me to the beat our hips were creating, there was nothing else but him.

His tongue slid into me, followed by his hips, while he fitted his entire body against mine. He wasn't only making love to me—he was possessing me.

There was nothing I wanted more than him, nothing I wouldn't be willing to sacrifice. Nothing my life felt more dependent on than this man moving inside me.

He separated his mouth from mine, and his heavy breath came just outside my ear. I could feel the sheen of sweat covering his face, mixing with mine.

He moved inside me again, deeper this time. I almost screamed. I was so close I didn't think I could last. "I'm not letting you go, Luce," he whispered, his voice tight. "I won't let you leave. You're mine," he breathed, sinking his teeth into my ear as his hips flexed against mine once more.

And that was it. My body trembled against his, my hand reaching for the metal bed rail to brace myself. He continued moving inside me, his beat quickening as my body clenched around him. His hand joined mine as he followed me down the forgetting-reality path, his fingers wove through mine, squeezing them before his body collapsed against mine.

"Damn, Luce," he said, his head rising and falling against my chest.

My thoughts exactly. "How do you feel?" I asked, trying to bring my heart rate down. My heart wasn't having any of it. "How's your head?"

"My head's fine," he said, winding his arms around my back. "It's my goddamn heart that's about ready to bust something."

I started laughing, feeling as close to euphoria as a snarky, natural pessimist could. He joined in, his laughter vibrating against me.

And then the door burst open as the kind-faced nurse rushed in, her expression lined with concern.

Her eyes landed on the machine first, then on Jude, who

was resting bare-ass naked over me. The worry lines faded from her face. She looked at us with a parental expression. Walking over to the monitor, she shut the screaming thing off, then turned and headed for the door.

"At least you died and went to heaven," she said in an amused tone before she left us to it.

"Yes," Jude said into my chest, his laughter dimming. "I most certainly did."

"Too bad our little stint in heaven didn't last a little longer," I said, running my fingers over his head.

His body tensed in my hold as I felt that smile curve into the side of my breast. "Who says we can't make a return trip?" he said, lifting himself over me again.

I didn't have a chance to reply with my answer—reality—before his mouth and body moved into mine again.

SIXTEEN

*J*ude was sleeping the slumber of a happy man beside me. His crooked smile still rested on his face, but his arms held me tight. Even after a second handrail-bracing, body-trembling, grit-your-teeth-around-a-scream roll in a hospital bed, I hadn't been able to fall asleep.

Jude had no trouble. In fact, my heartbeat hadn't recovered fully before he'd fallen asleep. I'd been awake for six hours, staring at the man curled around me, more confused than I'd ever been before. How could we be wrong for each other after making love just proved how very right we were for each other? And why, no matter what we seemed to do, didn't things work out for us?

My flight out of Syracuse was leaving in less than two hours. I didn't have my bag with me, and there would be no way I'd be able to drive to my dorm to get it and make it back before my plane had already landed in sunny south Arizona.

Thankfully, when I'd booked the ticket last month, I had guessed I'd be at Jude's game the Saturday before I flew out and planned on staying at his place that night. My plans certainly hadn't factored in a hospital bed, or clenched fingers running down cool metal bed rails, but if I left now, at least I could still make my flight.

I couldn't wake him. I couldn't let him know I was leaving, because he wouldn't let me go. Or he'd buy a ticket and come along with me.

And one part of me very much wanted that to happen. But the confused part of me, the one that was scratching her head in wonder, contemplating what to do next, needed some time and space to work out this new complication in what was becoming the never-ending tale of Jude and me.

More time and space.

I sighed, shifting in bed, trying to move myself from beneath him. This past month's "time and space" had done nothing but further confuse me and complicate things between the two of us. So I vowed I would force myself to make a decision by the time I returned to New York after the New Year. Before I came back to Syracuse, I would be able to give Jude a firm and final answer to the question that was our relationship.

Tucking the sheet around him, I herded up my clothes, jamming my neck and limbs into all the appropriate openings. Grabbing my bag from the table, I paused at the foot of the bed and stared at him. I couldn't seem to stop. He was mine. I knew this with all my heart.

But could I have him?

I wouldn't rest until I could answer this question.

I didn't dare run my fingers over the tips of his toes for fear of him waking up and convincing me back into bed. I rushed out the door, careful to close it without a sound.

I took the stairs, dodging the elevators by the nurses' station because I didn't want to explain myself. I couldn't explain anything right now. Other than that I was confused as all hell.

Once I was outside the hospital, I had a line of cabs to choose from. Sliding inside the closest one, I glanced back at the hospital, my eyes shifting to the fifth floor.

"The airport, please," I said, narrowing my eyes to focus better on the window I was looking into. A shadow suddenly moved away from it. "And please hurry," I added, the ball re-forming in my throat.

The cabdriver followed my request to a speed-defying

T. In fact, he put NYC cabdrivers to shame. Less than a half hour after we'd left the hospital, we were pulling up to Syracuse Hancock International Airport.

I hurried my way to the electronic ticket counters, wanting to get off the ground as soon as possible. I couldn't think clearly in New York.

Ticket in hand, I got in line at the security checks. On Christmas Eve, I expected to see more grumpy-faced people and screaming children. Before I'd had time to catch my breath, I was being ushered toward the metal detector.

Throwing my purse, phone, and boots onto the conveyor belt, I whisked through. I breathed a sigh of relief when it didn't beep. Last time I'd flown, I'd forgotten to take off my chunky sterling silver necklace, and I'd had to endure an intense "pat-down" from one very eager, very young male agent. I'd been the high point of his day as he'd been the low point of mine.

As I snatched my belongings at the end of the conveyor belt, I heard it.

Well, I heard him.

"Lucy!"

My head snapped up. I couldn't see him yet, but I could hear him like he was standing in front of me. The agents and others around me stopped what they were doing to look too.

"Lucy!" This time it sounded closer. Sure enough, Jude

emerged from around the corner, in full sprint, barefoot, and his hospital gown streaming around him. His eyes latched onto me like they were programmed to find nothing else.

"Lucy!" he repeated, charging the security gates. TSA agents were racing over.

He didn't stop sprinting, taking out one, then two rows of nylon people-herders. He didn't stop until a couple of large agents tackled him.

"Stop!" I screamed. "Don't hurt him!" Even in my panic, I knew they weren't the ones who were hurting him right now. My hands covered my mouth as the guards stopped him, each one grabbing an arm and throwing it behind him. Jude didn't fight back; he just stared at me with those dark eyes, pleading with me to stay.

"Don't leave, Luce!" he hollered. He only resisted when the guards tried to remove him from the security area.

"I'm just going away for a little while," I said, not sure whether he could hear me, since I couldn't seem to manage more than a whisper. "I'll be back. I promise."

"You can't leave me," he said, his voice breaking, his face following me as the guards pulled him away. This time, successfully. "You can't leave me," he said one last time, defeated.

"I'm not leaving you, Jude," I said, more to myself than to him. "I'm setting you free."

I don't know what was worse: watching Jude give up and be dragged away or turning away from him and heading for my gate.

Both ate at me until my plane landed in Arizona, and I wasn't sure if anything was left of the old Lucy Larson.

SEVENTEEN

*C*hristmas came and went without me so much as noticing. Well, I noticed. You couldn't help but notice when your entire extended family talked over one another like it was an Olympic sport. My ears were ringing an hour into the evening. I wasn't exactly a wallflower, but in the Larson family's company, I was the definition of one. I don't think I got two whole sentences out before everyone left for the night.

Life didn't make sense anymore. Or maybe I was about to stop trying to make sense of it for the first time.

I curled up in Grandpa's old recliner, staring out at the cacti twinkling with Christmas lights, trying to imagine what Jude was doing at that exact minute. Experiencing a moment of weakness, I slipped my phone out of my pocket and typed, MERRY CHRISTMAS. XXX&O and pressed send before

I could rethink it. I waited up most of the night, checking my screen for a reply.

Nothing.

More sleepless nights.

More days I tried to pass at the nearby dance studio when I needed a break from thinking about Jude.

On New Year's Day morning, I zombie-walked into the kitchen, beelining for the coffeepot.

"And I thought I was the insomniac in the family."

I didn't even startle, I was that sleep deprived. Mom rose from her chair at the table and walked over to the cupboard where Grandma kept her coffee cups. She poured a cup for me, adding the milk without asking.

"Thanks," I yawned as she set the cup in front of me.

"You're welcome," she said, sitting back down and watching me, as if she was waiting for something.

With my mom, nothing was ever as it seemed. She might be waiting for me to share my every goal and dream with her or she might be about to tell me that swept-off-the-face hairstyle I'd been favoring lately wasn't a good look for my heart-shaped face.

I'd burned through half a cup of coffee before she cleared

ally done waiting for you to open up about otten you so down," she said. "What's going on with you, Lucille? I know it has something to do with you and Jude. I just can't figure out what it is."

I cringed first over her use of my given name and winced when she said Jude's name. It hurt me just to hear it.

I sighed, taking a deep chug of coffee before setting it down.

"I'm not sure if we're supposed to be together," I said, offering nothing else. This was, at the core of all my concerns, the big one.

My mom nodded her head, taking a few moments to think before replying. "You're not sure if you're supposed to be together, or if you shouldn't be together?"

My brain wasn't working well enough to have this kind of conversation. "Is there a difference?"

"Of course," she said, cinching the belt of her new bathrobe tighter. "To suppose is to assume. Should is an entirely different beast. Should implies duty and obligation. It's a period where suppose is a question mark," she said, watching me across the table. "So yes, there's a difference."

Yep, I should have stayed in bed and continued to toss and turn. That would have been better than having this conversation with my mom before the crack of dawn.

"I guess I don't know?" I said.

"You want to know what I think?" Mom asked, her voice and face showing concern.

251

"Sure," I said, needing some solid Mom advice. In the months that followed my senior year, we'd managed to rebuild a good part of the relationship we'd lost after my brother's death. I gave a little, she gave a little, and somewhere along the way, we found a middle ground that worked for us. She didn't want to lose her daughter, her *only* child, and I didn't want to lose my mom. It was a breakthrough I never thought would happen, but I was thankful it had.

Now she even snuck a few napkin notes into the care packages she and Dad sent me at school.

"From an outsider's perspective, you and Jude probably aren't supposed to be together," she began slowly, watching my face for my reaction. "But at the same time, you two should be together."

I shook my head, trying to clear it. I couldn't keep up. This whole conversation seemed like one giant oxymoron.

"Okay, Mom. That was clear as mud," I said, narrowing my eyes as the start of a headache emerged. "Are you saying we *should* or *shouldn't* be together?"

"You should," she answered immediately.

Glad that was cleared up, and even though I wanted further clarification on the whole should/suppose mind maze, I couldn't do that to myself without bringing on a migraine.

"How can you be so sure of that when I'm not?"

"Honey," she said, patting my hand. "You're letting the

fairy tales you grew up with cloud your mind. Love isn't easy. Especially the really good kind. It's difficult, and you'll want to rip your hair out just as many days as you'll feel the wind at your back." She paused, smiling to herself. "But it's worth it. It's worth fighting for. Don't let what isn't real blind you to what is. Life isn't perfect, we aren't perfect, so why should we expect love to be?"

"I get that, I do. But come on, Mom," I said, trailing my finger along the rim of my cup. "Love just isn't enough sometimes."

"Baby," she said, looking at me like I'd just said something very immature, "I'd sign my name in blood that it isn't."

I groaned, sinking into my chair. This little mother/daughter convo was getting me nowhere.

"I'm so damn confused right now, Mom. I'm so confused I don't think anything you could say or explain would clear it all up for me."

She stayed silent for a minute, her forehead lining along with the corners of her eyes.

"Love is what brings you together, Lucy. But it's the blood, sweat, and tears of hard work that keeps you together," she began, choosing her words carefully. "Love isn't just about flowers, candlelight, and romance, sweetheart. It's hard work, and trust, and tears, and misery. But at the end of each day, if you can still look at the person at your side and can't imagine anyone else you'd rather have there, the pain and heartache and the ups and downs of love are worth it."

And the clouds of confusion started to part.

"Love is just as much suffering as it is sweetness. If it was perfect, that's what they'd call it. They wouldn't call it bittersweet."

"Are you saying every relationship experiences the same kinds of highs and lows Jude and I do?" I asked, taking another sip of coffee. "Because I think more people would choose to be alone if that was the case."

"Lucy, you're a passionate, emotional person. So is Jude. What do you expect to be the result when you two come together? You two don't multiply the peaks and the valleys together; you exponentially affect them," she said, getting up and grabbing the coffeepot from the holder.

"And there's no doubt that for some people, life would be far easier if they never fell in love. If they never had to ache for a man like he was their yesterday, today, and tomorrow." She filled my cup, then hers, before settling the pot between us. Gauging my mom's love-a-thon lecture here, we'd drain it soon. "Life would be smoother and you'd know more what to expect from day to day if you kept love out of your life." She paused, looking at the window as the first rays of dawn started shining through. "But you'd be alone."

"So you're saying I should choose Jude over a life of hermitlike solitude?" I asked, lifting my brows at her.

"I'm saying you should choose Jude if, at the end of the day, when the world is against you, you can say with absolute certainty that you want him at your side. Can you say the good times are worth the bad times?"

My body and mind were becoming more alert as the caffeine pulsed through my veins. After weeks of worry and uncertainty, I could finally make up my mind.

About time.

"When did you become Jude's number one fan?" I asked, smiling over at her. Mom had gone from loathing Jude when we first met, to disliking him through the entirety of my senior year, to tolerating him since we'd been together in college. I hadn't realized she'd crossed into the land of Jude approval.

"When he showed again and again that he's on your side," she answered simply. "I can forgive a man's past faults, his present shortcomings, and his future failures if every minute of every day he loves me like it's his religion," she said, taking a breath. "Jude loves you like that. It just took me a while to see that. So, yes, he's got the Mom stamp of approval now."

I didn't reply, my mind was so hard at work. I wasn't

255

so much rethinking things, as realigning expectations and assumptions and even a bit of my worldview. I'd been so focused on the reasons Jude and I shouldn't be together, I'd been blinded to the reasons we should. And now that I'd "seen the light," it was becoming clear that those reasons were worth every bit of hardship that came our way.

"Working things out over there, sweetheart?" Mom said, startling me. I'd gone so far and long down the paths of my thoughts, everything had faded away.

I took a slow breath, feeling the confidence drown away all the doubt. "All worked out, I think," I said. "Thanks, Mom. For the coffee, for listening, and for the 'come to Jude' talk."

"You're welcome, Lucy," she said, arching a brow as she studied me. "But what in the world are you still doing in that chair?"

My eyes squinted—was she saying what I thought she was?

Waving her hand at the back door, she said, "Go get your man. Go be happy and miserable together."

Yep.

EIGHTEEN

Flying on New Year's Day had its advantages. Next to no one else was traveling, so I had no problem getting my return ticket changed to the very next flight, which left in an hour. When I started blabbering out my whole life story to the poor lady behind the ticket counter, she gave me a knowing smile and upgraded me to first class.

A coffee stand was positioned right next to my gate, so by the time they called my flight, I was really buzzing like a live wire.

First class was everything people raved about. The seats were twice as big and at least ten times as comfortable. The flight attendants were eager to meet your every request. It was high rolling at thirty thousand feet.

All the luxury aside, I don't think my foot stopped tapping once the entire flight.

I was the first person off the plane when those doors opened at Syracuse Hancock International Airport, and I was in a full run by the time I hit the terminal. I had to haul ass to the stadium, because kickoff was in less than an hour.

"The Carrier Dome, please," I said, breathing like I was trying to take off. "And if it wasn't a matter of love and life, I wouldn't be begging you right now to break every traffic rule to get there as fast as we can in one piece. Preferably in one piece," I added.

The cabdriver glanced back at me over his shoulder. His face was familiar. "Why are you in such a hurry to get everywhere you go?" he asked, slipping his sunglasses over his eyes. "Haven't you ever been told to enjoy the journey?"

"I'll enjoy the journey once I get there," I answered, thanking my lucky stars I'd crashed into this cab. This guy had driven me here on my first trip in record time; it was fitting that he drove me again now.

He smirked as he pulled away from the curb. "What's the damn rush?"

I smirked right back. "I've got to apologize to, plead with, and make sweet love to the man I love," I answered, buckling in. "Now make this yellow hunk of junk move!"

He rested his head back and laughed. "Lucky for you I like bossy women," he said, unleashing that yellow hunk of junk loose on the road.

This time, as the cars and scenery blurred by me, I feared for my life. I guess finally deciding on the life you wanted to live made it more valuable.

As we braked to a stop at the curb outside the ticket windows, I shoved some bills into his hand and slid out of the door. "You are a god among cabbies, my friend," I said.

He chuckled like it was cute of me to acknowledge what he already knew.

"Good luck," he said before I slammed the door shut.

I knew this would be the last chance for one good deep breath, so I took it, holding it inside, sucking all the courage and kismet I could from it before letting it go. Turning around, I rushed toward the gates, where my favorite ticket master waited behind the window.

"Miss Lucy!" His face lit up. "I wasn't sure you'd make it. Cutting it a little close, aren't you, kiddo?" he said, checking the clock over his shoulder.

"How you feeling today, Lou?" I asked, knowing my plan was going to fall flat on its face without his help.

"Old, arthritic," he began, eyeing me, "and spry and ornery as the day I was born."

I exhaled my relief. "Good," I said. "I need a favor."

Lou's face flattened in surprise before, looking from side to side at the other employees around him, he leaned across the counter, his eyes gleaming. "I hope it's a good one."

My hands were sweating. Not clammy, not damp. Sweaty.

Every part of my body seemed to have grown sweat glands that were dripping liquid like I was going through some purification ritual in a steam hut.

Not to be excluded, my heart was about to burst from my chest, and my knees were seriously checking themselves out of the game. If my mind wasn't so made up, so firm in its endeavor, my body would give out beneath me.

"You won't have long, Miss Lucy," Lou whispered over to me, handing me a cordless microphone.

"I won't need long," I answered, my foot tapping making its reappearance when I peered into the stands. Where the airports were next to empty on New Year's Day, the bleachers at college football stadiums were packed to capacity. And I was about to go out in front of all that.

Shit. Hopefully, I would be more articulate when I wandered onto that field and put that mike to use.

"Do you know how to work one of these things?" he asked, eyeing the mike in my hands. It was slippery from my sweaty hands, so now, in addition to not tripping, not fainting, and not saying anything stupid, I had to add "don't let the mike slide from my hands" to the punch card.

"Slide to on," I recited, my voice shaking too. "Hold to mouth. Try not to sound like a blubbering idiot."

Lou gave me his warm smile.

"I happen to be partial to blubbering idiots," he said, resting his hand on my shoulder. "My wife was one, and I swear, that's what won me over. She had to say everything that was on her mind without putting it through a filter." Those brown eyes of his took on a faint sheen. "Five years later, after she passed, that's what I lie in bed missing the most."

Wrapping my arms around him, I gave Lou a shaky, sweaty hug which he seemed to melt into. When I pulled away, he wiped at his eyes.

"Mr. Jude's a very lucky man," he said, backing away.

I smiled after him. "I didn't exactly draw the short stick."

"No, hon, you sure didn't," he said, nodding his head toward the field. "Go get him."

"Okay," I said, feeling like I was about to throw up.

"When you're ready, just give your head a nod, and I'll make sure that mike streams all the way to the parking lot."

I flashed him a thumbs-up because my nerves were clenching at my throat.

As I peered into the stands, another wave of nausea rolled over me. The teams were about to take the field. Lou had assured me whether Jude was in the locker room, or in the tunnel, or on the field, there would be no way in hell he couldn't hear my voice coming through the speakers.

Along with fifty thousand others.

It was hard enough to contend with vulnerability, not to mention a crapload of impartial strangers witnessing my big confession. But this was what I had to do. I'd put him through hell these past few months, and he'd willingly walked through the fire, knowing he'd get burned. It had taken losing him, feeling like I was losing myself, and losing him one more time, for me to figure out just what I wanted. And that was Jude. No matter what came my way, if Jude was at my side, life would be good.

I knew that what I was about to do wouldn't make up for what I'd put him through. Nothing could do that, but I hoped this grand gesture would appeal to that soft spot he'd always had for me. Jude had put himself out there so many times before, not caring what others thought about him and the way he felt about me. Now it was my turn. I was the one who had much to atone for.

And atonement was one short walk to the fifty-yard line.

I closed my eyes, visualizing Jude's face. His many faces. The one that burst into laughter when I tried to be tough, the one that had smoothed into a smile when I'd told him I loved him, the one that had broken when I'd walked away too many damn times. And finally, the one of acceptance I hoped I'd find waiting for me when I said what needed to be said.

With renewed resolve, I opened my eyes and took my first step onto the field. I held my breath, hoping no one would tackle me or Taser me when they noticed I didn't have a badge swinging from my neck, but no one seemed to pay much attention to the girl wandering to the fifty with a mike in her hand.

My hands were shaking by the twenty, and the rest of me by the thirty. But as I took my final steps to the fifty, I was in the Zen zone. I'd jumped—that was the hard part—now all I had to do was enjoy the free fall.

Holding the mike up, I scanned the crowd. People were starting to shift their attention my way. I pretended they were checking out the water boys on the sidelines. Glancing toward the dark tunnel, I gave a nod of my head.

The mike buzzed to life. I flinched in surprise. It was the first time I'd held one of these things and hadn't anticipated that. Dancing didn't require microphones.

"Hello?" I said, cementing my spot for the idiot-of-the-year award. Was I expecting someone to greet me back? My voice blazed around the stadium.

Now, I'd gotten everyone's attention. Including the tall, broad guys with black tees that read SECURITY across their backs.

Lou was right. I'd have to be fast.

"My name's Lucy," I began, my voice breaking. I cleared it.

Just pretend you're talking to no one else but Jude.

"And once upon a time I fell in love with this guy." The stadium went silent as everyone took their seats for the Lucy Larson Gut-Spilling Show. "He wasn't exactly a fairy-tale prince. But I'm no fairy-tale princess." I paused, reminding myself to breathe. This would all be for nothing if I passed out from oxygen deprivation. "He didn't ride in on a white horse or say all the right things at just the right time. But he was my prince. He would have been the Prince Charming I wrote about if I wrote fairy tales."

I noticed a couple of security guards reach for their walkie-talkies, mumbling something into them with stern faces. *Hurry, Lucy.*

"That man made me feel things I never imagined could

be felt. He made me want things I wasn't sure I could have. He made me need things I didn't know I needed."

My voice was getting stronger as the words started spilling from me. Everything I'd needed to say for so long was finally having its day.

"He made me happy. He made me crazy. He made me thank the heavens for the day I'd met him. He made me curse the same heavens for the day I'd met him." I smiled, a slew of memories flashing through my mind.

"I screwed up. He screwed up. I was sure I couldn't live without him. I was just as sure he'd be the death of me. I was *confused*." Straddling the fifty, I completed one revolution, waiting for number seventeen to come running across the field to me.

No smiling faces.

I had more to make up for. I only hoped it would be enough.

"We rode this roller coaster. Up, down, and around and around, and just as soon as I was sure it was coming to a stop and we could get off it once and for all, we repeated the same ride all over again. I didn't think I wanted to be a passenger on that ride anymore, so I got off, leaving him to ride it alone."

A couple of guards nodded into their walkies before

pocketing them and coming onto the field for me. I did another survey of the field.

Where. Was. He?

"Then we shared one amazing night. I thought everything would be all right. And then doubt crept back into my mind, and I knew nothing would be all right. So I left him. Again. I hurt him." A single phantom tear slipped down my cheek.

I ignored the guards who were making their way toward me. I looked into the stands. I saw more sympathetic faces than judgmental ones.

It turns out, I wasn't the only one who screwed love up.

"But then this morning, after another sleepless night and a pot of coffee, someone knocked some sense into me. Thanks, Mom," I said, waving at the camera that was tracking me. "I realized I'd never really gotten off that roller coaster—we were just riding in different cars. My life is a roller coaster whether or not I am sitting next to this boy, and I'd rather share this crazy journey through life with him at my side."

Sucking in a deep breath, I busted into the finale, because I had maybe ten seconds before I would be escorted off the field. Hopefully not in cuffs.

"I'm done leaving. I'm done questioning if we can do this thing, Jude."

Cheering rose up in the stands as fans began to realize their star quarterback was who this screw-loose girl was talking about.

"I'm done pretending I'll ever love someone else as much as I love you. I know it took me a while, but I know it now. I was made to love you. I was made to share my life with you. I'm rewriting the fairy tale so you and I get to ride off together." I paused again to get a breath and scanned the field.

He wasn't coming. Even if he'd been tucked away into the very back of the stadium, he could have made it to me by now if he wanted to. Nothing stopped Jude from what he wanted. The possibility that I wasn't what he wanted anymore broke me.

I fought through the fear. I was done living in a state of it.

"I love you, Jude Ryder. I'm done letting that scare me. I'm not going anywhere."

One of the security guards stopped in front of me, clearing his throat. "Yes, ma'am. I'm afraid you are."

This was so not how I'd envisioned all this going. I gave life, smirking its all-knowing face at me, the finger.

"I'll take that," he said, grabbing the mike out of my hands. "After you," he said, motioning me off the field.

The other guard shouldered up next to me, waiting for me as well. At least neither one was swinging a pair of cuffs in front of me. Taking one more look around the field, I felt my already battered heart break one final time.

It was done—it couldn't break any more than it just had. If Jude didn't want it, I didn't need it anyway.

Making myself hold my head high, I followed behind one of the guards, the other one keeping stride beside me as I left the field. The stadium was silent again as I felt the eyes of every person watching me being escorted from the field where I'd just bared my soul.

Where I'd left it there to die.

My future was flashing through my mind as we crossed into the dark tunnel, looking bleak and empty. My future, Judeless, wasn't one I looked forward to waking up to every day.

I was midway through the tunnel, at the point where it was darkest, when something buzzed to life in the stadium. It startled me just as much as it had the first time. The two guards froze right along with me, but their mouths didn't curve into smiles like mine did.

"Lucy Larson?" That voice I couldn't possibly love any more without being declared mentally unstable rose through the stadium. "Could you come back out here? I need to ask you something."

The guards groaned. I almost squealed I was so giddy,

and Lucy Larson did not normally do giddy.

"Ready to make this a round trip, boys?" I said.

As I hurried out of the tunnel, the light of the stadium blinded me for a moment, but then a flash of orange and white decorating the fifty-yard line cleared my vision. Jude straddled that line, his helmet at his feet, and his eyes nowhere else but on me.

His face gave nothing away, but I didn't care if he was out there to chastise me in front of everyone or if he was planning on making sweet love to me right there on the field. I wasn't turning my back on him again.

I told myself to walk, to put one foot in front of the other, but I couldn't. I started running. Fifty yards had never felt so far away, and I had never wanted anything as much as what I wanted at the end of those fifty yards.

The crowd wasn't silent anymore. People were cheering. But the only thing I noticed was the man who was watching me with such intensity that I could feel it coming off him in waves.

Slowing to a jog, I stopped before throwing myself into his arms. Because, for one of the few times ever, Jude's arms weren't open out to me.

"That was one hell of a speech, Luce," he said, his face finally breaking into a smirk. Almost identical to the one he'd given me that day on the beach when he'd crashed into me.

"I was wondering how far you'd let me get," I said, feeding him back his line from our beach-day meeting.

When I'd fallen for a broken boy who had managed to fix me somewhere along the way.

"How far do you think you had until you hit the edge of the world?" he replied, his smirk deepening.

"I'd say I fell over it a ways ago," I answered, knowing I'd fallen so long ago I couldn't remember when my feet had been planted on solid ground.

Jude stepped closer to me, resting one hand on my hip. "Then it's a damn good thing you grabbed onto that rope I told you we'd need when the ground fell out."

I smiled as his expression softened.

"Damn good thing, indeed," I said, feeling the warmth from his hand melt away whatever confusion or uncertainty or doubt was left. "Didn't you say you had something to ask me?" I arched a brow, scanning the crowd and the cameras aimed at us. "Because I'd say we've got five more seconds before they send for the SWAT team."

Jude blew out a breath, that foreign flash in his eyes looking . . . *nervous*?

"I wasn't planning on doing it this way," he said into the

microphone, one side of his mouth curling up, "but I suppose that's par for our course, Luce."

"Did that concussion knock something loose?" I teased, amused at this bout of discomfort rolling off him.

"No, I still see everything as clearly as I did before," he answered, tugging on a chain around his neck. "And it's about time you saw it, too."

Throwing the microphone to the side, he stepped back. The crowd exploded into an equal chorus of cheers and boos.

Then, taking a deep breath, Jude lowered himself down to the field. On one knee.

Damn. My knees were about to join his.

He slid the chain over his head. A ring dangled from the end of it.

"I know I'm one royal screwup, and God knows there's nothing I could ever do to deserve you," he began, taking my hand in his after sliding the ring free from the chain. I couldn't fill my lungs, I couldn't feel my legs below me, but I could feel his hand in mine. And he kept me grounded.

"But I want you, Lucy Larson. Bad. I want you forever. The kind of bad I have for you isn't the kind that goes away." His forehead lined, his eyes washing silver. "Ease my suffering. Make me the happiest, most tortured man in the world. Marry me?"

Jude Ryder. The man I loved. The man I couldn't live without. My *husband*.

Yeah, that worked.

"Why the hell not," I answered, never feeling more sure about anything.

His face showed relief. And pure, unbridled joy.

"Was that a yes?" he asked, already sliding the ring onto my finger. I hadn't looked at the ring once. I could feel it there, the metal band cool on my skin, but I didn't need to see it to feel its promise. It could have been a hundred carats; it could have come from a quarter machine. I didn't care.

Because I had Jude.

Forever.

"No," I answered him, tugging on his hand, pulling him up. "That was a what-took-you-so-long, Ryder. That was a one-hundred-million-percent yes. Now get up here and kiss me." I winked down at him, grinning at me like a fool.

He popped up, and his arms grabbed me, folding me tightly against him. "Yes, ma'am."

As I wrapped my legs around him, he lifted me higher, weaving his fingers through my hair. "The name's Jude Ryder, since you're going to be my wife someday soon. And I didn't used to do girlfriends, flowers, or dates. And then I met you, and that didn't work for you. So I changed for you. And you changed for me too," he said, taking me back in time and keeping me right here in the present. And as I looked into his eyes and felt my lips on his, I felt the future too. It was surreal. The real kind that few people experienced. And here I was, living it. Lifting his lips from mine, he ran his knuckles down my face. "And we worked out something special."

"We didn't just work out something special," I replied, pressing a kiss into the corner of his mouth. "We worked ourselves a miracle."

AND CHECK OUT THE NEXT BOOK IN THE SERIES,

CRUSH!

*U*p, down. Round and around. Rinse and repeat. That was our pattern. That was our world.

With a guy like Jude Ryder at my side, the lows in life were lower and the highs were higher. This was our reality, our story . . . our *love* story. We fought; we made up. We messed up; we apologized. We lived; we learned. Jude and I had made a lot of mistakes in the history of our relationship, but one thing we always seemed to get right? Our all-consuming love for each other.

This was my life.

And you know what?

Life was pretty damn good.

Even despite the fact that I had no clue where I was.

"What are you up to?" I whispered back to Jude, continuing to let him lead me into the black hole.

"Something you'll love," he replied, squeezing my shoulders as he steered me along. My heels began to echo around me.

So we were in a tunnel, but what tunnel was totally beyond me, because Jude had made me close my eyes the moment I'd answered the door this evening. Other than driving around in his ancient rumble-wagon of a truck for the better part of a Friday date night, I'd lost my bearings in every way a girl could ever lose them.

Given the fact that Jude Ryder was my fiancé, my bearings had been a tad off-kilter for the past few years, but they were especially off the grid tonight.

Did this tunnel have an end? The longer we continued down it, the louder my footsteps echoed around us.

"Is whatever you're up to illegal?" I asked, not sure I really wanted to know.

"Is that a trick question?" he said, sounding amused.

"Is that a trick answer?"

He didn't respond immediately. Instead, I felt his mouth warm the skin at the base of my neck. One full breath out, and one full breath in, slow and deep and suffocating, before his lips grazed the heated patch of skin.

I tried not to react like his touch was hardwired to drive every bit of me crazy, but even after years together, Jude could still unravel me with one touch. My skin was pricking to life with tiny goose bumps that trailed down to my lower back when his mouth pulled away.

"There will most certainly be high points tonight that could be classified as illegal in every one of the Bible Belt states," he said, his voice low with desire. Not quite as rough as it got when he needed me right then and there; it was still restrained enough that I knew he wasn't going to throw me up against the nearest wall and start fisting up my skirt before we got a step farther. "Does that answer your question?"

"No," I said, trying to sound controlled. Trying to sound like he hadn't made my stomach clench with desire from one kiss. "It doesn't answer my question. So let's try this again . . ." I cleared my throat, reminding myself I was trying to sound unaffected. "In whatever never-ending hallway you're leading me down, toward whatever location you're aiming to wind up at, could either one of these trespasses be considered illegal if we were to be tried in court?"

He didn't make a noise, but I knew he was trying to contain a chuckle. One of those low, rumbling ones that vibrated through my body when he was pressed up against me. "Since you put it that way . . ." he started, stopping me suddenly. His hands left my shoulders and tapped my eyelids. "Yes. It could be. However," he said, "they'd have to catch us first. Open your eyes, babe."

I blinked my eyes a few times to make sure what I was seeing was real.

After another half dozen blinks, I could be reasonably certain that what my eyes were taking in was, in fact, real.

We were inside the Carrier Dome, just at the mouth of one of the tunnels. However, this was the dome like I'd never seen it in the past three years of attending almost every home game. At the center of the field, right at the fifty, a blanket was spread out, and what looked like a picnic basket rested in one corner. A smattering of white candles in clear jars were dotted around the blanket. It was still, silent, and peaceful.

Not the first three words you'd usually use to describe a college football arena.

And this wasn't the place a girl expected her fiancé would take her on a big surprise date he'd wanted her to get dressed up for.

I grinned.

Not what I'd expected, but exactly what I wanted.

"What do you think? This worth 'illegal'?" he asked, winding his arms around my waist and tucking his chin over my shoulder.

I couldn't take my eyes off the candlelit scene in front of me. A picnic on the fifty-yard line.

I knew it might not have ranked in the top-ten desired

dates for most girls, but it hit the number-one spot for this girl.

"It's only illegal if we get caught," I answered, turning my head so he could see my smile, before breaking free of his arms and jogging over to the blanket.

This was the first time I'd been down on the field since Jude and I got engaged our freshman year of college, but it really did seem like it had been only a handful of days ago. I'd discovered another one of life's clichés by being with Jude: The happier you are in life, the faster it passes you by. Life was one sick bastard if happy people were repaid with a life that seemed short. Short life or long life, it didn't matter—I wasn't giving up Jude either way.

At the twenty-five-yard line, I spun around, continuing to jog backward. Jude was still at the mouth of the tunnel, watching me with a grin, appearing as enamored by me as he had on the day he'd confessed his love. That look, more than any of the others, got to me in all the ways a guy's look was supposed to "get" to his girl.

I perused the stands one more time to make sure we were alone. It felt so damn open in here, which was unnerving, but how many times could a girl say she'd been with the number-one-ranked college quarterback in the nation right on the fifty-yard line?

Yeah, this was a once-in-a-lifetime deal, and I wasn't going to let it pass me by.

Inhaling a slow breath, I reached for the hem of my sweater and started sliding it up my stomach.

Jude's expression changed instantly. His forehead lined deeper and one corner of his mouth twitched.

Raising a brow, I lifted the rest of my sweater, tugging it over my head and dropping it onto the Astroturf. My adrenaline was pumping. The anticipation of having Jude with me set it off, and the thrill of being here was firing it to new heights.

Winding my arms behind my back, I unclasped my bra. It snapped free, sliding down my arms to join the sweater at my feet.

Jude wasn't looking at my face any longer.

Wetting his lips, he started toward me.

I started my backward journey again, flicking him a coy smile. I was going to have fun with him, draw this out. Get even with him for what he so often did to me.

He stopped as soon as I started moving away, staring at me like he knew exactly what game I was playing and he both loved and hated being a pawn in it.

Pausing just long enough to step out of my heels, I slid my thumbs under the waist of my skirt and lowered it down my hips, slowing just enough to gather the material of my panties with it. I let both skirt and underwear gather at my ankles.

Jude's eyes drifted lower, his chest rising and falling noticeably, even from where I stood thirty yards away from him. When his eyes did shift back to mine, they were dark with one thing.

Absolute need.

His body sprang to action as he burst onto the field after me, running at the same pace he did when he was playing a game. I turned and laughed with every step as I ran away from him.

It was a futile effort, running from Jude—both right now, and in life in general.

Jude always caught up with me. Sometimes he gave me a head start, but he never let me get too far.

READ THE REST OF
CRUSH
AS AN EBOOK OR PAPERBACK!